Castles
and
Cowsheds

Castles
and
Cowsheds

FAITH LAWRENCE

Matador
9 Priory Business Park,
Wistow Road, Kibworth Beauchamp,
Leicestershire. LE8 0RX
Tel: 0116 279 2299
Email: books@troubador.co.uk
Web: www.troubador.co.uk/matador
Twitter: @matadorbooks

ISBN 978 1784625 252

British Library Cataloguing in Publication Data.
A catalogue record for this book is available from the British Library.

Printed and bound by CPI Group (UK) Ltd, Croydon, CR0 4YY
Typeset in 11pt Aldine401 BT by Troubador Publishing Ltd, Leicester, UK

Matador is an imprint of Troubador Publishing Ltd

MIX
Paper from
responsible sources
FSC
www.fsc.org
FSC® C013604

To my beloved family

20th February 1832.

Father Thomas Doyle wrote to the Editor of the London Times.

"Sir, In mercy and as a friend of the suffering and deserted poor, do say something for the Irish poor of Southwark. Many of these poor have no bed to lie on; they sleep at night on the floor – an unfurnished room, without fire, without clothes, without food, without hope in this world."

Years ago Dr Poynter of St Edmund's College, Ware, had spoken to one of his students.

"You are a fine organist but there is a dearth of priests in England. I think you should be ordained in 1819. People are desperate for help in South London. There is a chapel in Southwark, a little wooden shack, and thousands of worshippers. You would be about twenty-six years of age and that should be ideal."

Young Doyle agreed to this new way of life.

Dr Poynter said, "You have always been a little over-ambitious, but I know you will do everything possible to help the people, young or old, rich or poor. You remember the story of the Gordon Riots? They were on the fields nearby in 1780. Gordon fought the Catholics and I believe about 60,000 people were killed, some in battle. Many were neither Catholic nor Protestant. This will be your territory. You will be very, very busy – the Chaplains are obliged to attend Guy's and St Thomas's Hospitals, at the King's Bench, the Surrey, the Marshalsea and the Clink Prisons. There are about four workhouses and about 7,000 persons. These are chiefly poor labourers and their families or widows and orphans."

Years later Father Thomas became the first Chaplain of St George's. His idea of a new church burgeoned from 1833-40. 1852. There was an appeal in the Notice Book.

"Now, near the Victoria Theatre, there lies a human being whose exterior was once very agreeable but much sickness and trouble have changed her sadly. Her little back room was ever the same for two years past – silent, cheerless, and herself always sick in the head and heart, and invariably in bed.

Poor woman! Half of her body is, as it were, dead and a combination of diseases feed on her attenuated frame. She cannot lie down, she cannot sit up. She cannot sleep, but still she lives.

Her son was killed; he was drowned two years ago at night. Her other son, who was a cripple but meant everything to her, was moved to Lambeth Workhouse to die.

The young man used to sell things on the street and did all that an affectionate son could for a mother. He cleaned the little street, made the fire and the tea, waited upon her as a nurse, and cheered her and soothed her troubled heart.
Now he is dead and God help her. The remains of her son lie in the workhouse coffin rested at the foot of her bed.

If there be a heart of flesh within you send something to Father Thomas for the afflicted one." Later – "You are all very kind, and the poor working man with his half a crown."

The young priest, Father Thomas Doyle, was amazed when he saw the Belgian Chapel for the first time in his life. The little wooden shack could only hold two or three hundred people, worshipping the Lord Our God. Others gathered on the street outside, saying their prayers and trying to hear the service. The impoverished, deaf and blind.

He thought, The impoverished must have a church of their own. St George's Fields might become St George's Church, even St George's Cathedral?

Pipe dreams?

The year was 1819, long before the Irish famine that drove so many families to England and America, longing for food and wealth; escape from starvation and the cholera.

Father Thomas Doyle was a very determined man, born in England, the son of an Irish family.

"I will make it happen."

He wrote many letters to The Times and, from 1840, to the Catholic Tablet. Witty, amusing, with an agenda – to raise money and build a church.

Many Catholic men and women haunted the confessional to reveal their sins – theft, murder, work as pimps or prostitutes. Cock-fighting and bear-baiting were their pastimes. A few worked as mill hands, dockers and errand boys. All had stories to tell.

The Elephant And Castle

The stink of dead animals rose from the River Thames.

Stray cats and dogs. Rotten fish. Shit.

Felix Kelly blew his nose on an old rag and did a double somersault in the alleyway.

Clip-clop. A cart horse carried fruit and vegetables to the weekly market; a curricle was on its way to the George Inn. His dad, Jonathan, said that every other pub in the area was a brothel. Felix did not understand the word; he was only ten years of age.

An old woman emptied her piss-pot out of a window on to the street, narrowly missing the little boy.

Felix called out, "Bad shot, lady!"

The crone cackled and went back to sleep on the bare boards of her hovel.

Young Felix did another somersault near the stage door of the theatre at the Elephant and Castle. He slipped and fell on his bum in the gutter.

A glass eye glinted in the mud; a monocle winked at him. A Malacca cane lay nearby. One of the pros might have dropped them when he was as pissed as a newt in Paradise.

Daddy Jonathan always joked, "Drunk for a penny, dead drunk for tuppence."

Felix had never heard of the lyricist William Schwank Gilbert or Gilbert and Sullivan operas.

Felix did not know that Gilbert had written:

"Precocious baby who was born
A pipe in his mouth, and a glass in his eye
A hat all awry,
An octagon tie
And a miniature, miniature glass in his eye."

He picked up the props and swaggered towards the stage door of the South London Palace of Varieties. The theatre had been destroyed by fire and rebuilt in nine months in the shape of a Roman villa. The half-circle could now seat 4,000 people in the audience.

Felix was longing to see inside and this might be his only chance. He popped the monocle into his left eye and placed the cane on to his lean shoulder. *Might one become a pro at ten years of age?* He knew a little girl of four who sang and danced in Hyde Park Gardens.

The stage door keeper, a burly old man, leaned over him; Felix shoved the odds and sods forward.

"I found these on the street, Sir."

He heard a voice rise and fall; someone was rehearsing on stage. Felix joined in the Irish ballad … "singing cockles and mussels, alive alive-o."

The theatre chairman strolled towards him down a short passageway.

"Thank you for the props. I heard you sing, young man. Do you want to stand in the flies and watch the rehearsal?"

Felix laughed, "Stand in the flies! Do you have a bucket full of dead insects?"

"Don't be daft, boy. Come this way."

Felix watched the song and dance man and roared with laughter at a naughty comedienne. He was fascinated by a pianist on a grand piano.

The chairman eyed the young lad.

"Would you like to work in the theatre? You might help the dressers or become a call boy. I could pay you tuppence a week."

"Oh, yes please, Sir. That would be wonderful. I turned down an offer to be a rabbit-skinner and a cat-skinner 'cos I love animals. My name's Felix Kelly."

He ran all the way home to tell his mother, sister Rosa and brother Danny his Good Luck story.

The chairman turned to the bloke at the stage door.

"I think that kid will be a bill-topper, one day. He has the voice and the personality. God bless you, Felix."

★★★

Five and a half Kellys lived in a crumbling wooden shack close to the river. There were rows and rows of broken-down hovels near Lambeth Palace.

Mother Maria had warned the family: "There will soon be six of us; another little one is on the way. I don't know if it will be a boy or a girl."

Husband Jonathan piped up, "I don't give a damn; I shall bolt when it arrives. I could not bear to watch it pop out."

"You make it sound like a puppet."

Jonathan said, "It will be another mouth to feed, with watery bread and milk."

Felix was on the way home from the Elephant and Castle. He performed a cartwheel.

A slender crescent moon was peeping through the clouds.

His tummy was full, the man in the variety hall had said, "I expect you are hungry, kid. Have a nice cup of tea and some buns on the house. There's a bowl of soup if you fancy it."

Now he could see the glow from one candle shining

3

through the little broken window. The wooden door was jammed with an iron bar. He gave it a shove and nearly landed on his backside.

He could hear moans and groans; Kelly Number Six was on the way, into a world of bugs, lice and cockroaches.

There must be a better life for the young and poverty-stricken.

Kelly's Castle

Maria Kelly lay on the bare floor, her body curved like a brown snail. She waited for the next crippling pain.

Maria was half naked, clutching a moth-eaten piece of needlework to her breasts and belly. Her limbs were off-white, not sunburnt after the long summer, but grubby from the lack of clean water. There was a pump at the end of the alleyway; the privy pail was shared by all the family – Daddy Jonathan, Danny, Felix, Rosa and Mummy.

A low moan echoed through the hovel. A sheet of sopping wet cardboard flapped in the broken window frames. A sharp wind blew through the cracks in the door.

Maria shivered.

"Do be quiet, Mummy. I'm so tired, but I can't sleep when you are making all that noise." There was a knock on the front door, but they ignored it, knowing any intruders might be rapists or robbers.

"I've got the belly of a poisoned pup."

Maria Kelly patted her swollen tummy and rolled over on to all fours. "Wake up, Rosa, I need you."

A cockroach scuttled across the bare floorboards where she lay.

"I'm dying for a wee. Can you find me the privy pail?"

Her husband Jonathan was helping the cock handlers at the George Inn, getting ready for the next fight.

Little Rosa shivered under a grubby brown blanket.

Granddad would have gone berserk to see the family living in squalor after they sailed from Ireland. A broken down hovel in a Southwark back alley – without furniture, curtains or bedclothes.

Son Danny earned a penny or two running errands for the pubs and theatres.

The persecution, the famine and the cholera had affected so many of the poor Irish.

Maria groaned. "I think the baby's coming."

Rosa was wide awake now.

"I know it's getting dark, but if I light a candle bugs come out of the woodwork."

The front door was shoved open and a dark shadow appeared.

"Thank God."

It was son Felix, not a yobbo.

"I've been to the Elephant and Castle, the Palace of Varieties." He was longing to tell them his news but no one was listening. He flopped down on to a wooden crate covered with old newspapers rescued from the litter bins on the street, hoping to escape from the rats and mice that scuttled across the floor at night. The parents told him that spiders and ladybirds were lucky, but he cringed when he saw them.

A foul stink of sewage from the Thames seeped through the window, the glass was broken years ago.

"I think the baby's coming."

"Don't worry, Mummy. I've scrubbed the floorboards near the old fireplace and I put down Granny's woollen shawl. You can lie on that when you're ready."

Rosa was peering between her mother's legs. She had seen the birth of animals but never real live babies.

"I can see the little one's head popping out."

"Jesus, Mary and Joseph. Help me across the room, Rosa."
Felix had turned his back on them.

Maria caught her bare heels on the splintered wooden floor and fell sideways.

"Roll over, Mummy," Rosa said. "I saw a girl do this in a pub. I was looking through the window."

Felix chimed in, "You're a nosey parker."

Maria writhed in agony as the contractions came, faster and faster. A while later a piercing
shriek cleft the air. Danny, Felix, Rosa and now Lucia, the light at the end of the tunnel

"Get the pail to wash the little one. There will be a bloody mess on the floor. Is it a boy or a girl?"

"It's not come out yet. Here we go! I can't see a dangler."

"Another girl. Slap her on the bum when she gets here to make sure she's alive."

Maria was breathless and exhausted.

One day her new baby might work as a barmaid at the George Inn or The Prospect of Whitby at Wapping Old Stairs. God save us, there were so many dens of iniquity. She muttered a prayer for her baby.

Felix was gawping at last. "She's got a rope round her neck!"

The Ma said, "Cut the cord with a kitchen knife. Hold it tight to stop any bleeding, then tie a knot in it."

The bloody afterbirth slipped out of her body on to the bare floor.

Daddy Jonathan Kelly plodded over the cobblestones on his way home to high tea with his wife Maria, Danny, Felix and Rosa. Stale bread and cheese, again!

He wobbled, his old leather boots were worn down to the ground. His belly rumbled, he was starving hungry.

There was an outside chance the new baby might arrive

early. Money was even shorter than usual. They could not afford to celebrate the birth with a pot of ale, a drop if Irish whiskey, and lemonade for the kids. The pennies might stretch to milk from the market topped up with smelly water from the Thames!

Jonathan had nicked a lump of fruit cake from the kitchen of the George Inn when he was feeding the cocks. It was his temporary job several times a year.

He had always loved animals but today he had caught a rabbit. A ferret was chasing it down a hole at the riverside. The poor little beast would make a smashing stew, but he felt sick when he killed it.

He might be able to flog the bloody fur or dry it and make a winter bonnet for his wife, Maria. Otherwise one of his mates could use the pelt.

Lucia had fat, chubby cheeks and strands of dark hair, like her Daddy.

The colour of her eyes might change, from blue to hazel, brown or green.

Maria wrapped the little one in a scrap of old rag she had hidden from the rest of the family. They would have been fighting for it.

Maria stroked Lucia's pink paws and kissed the top of her head.

The mouth was a tiny rosebud.

The baby began to cry, louder and louder.

Rosa asked, "Shall I slap her bum and tell her to shut up?"

"Don't you dare. It's too late now; she's been in this world a little while."

Felix sang a lullaby and she fell asleep in her mother's arms.

Four children to feed and clothe and still try to lead the good life. God help us!

Pimps and street girls and the aristos were the only ones to earn a living, selling bodies, alive and dead.

★★★

Baby Lucia was baptised in St George's when she was only five days old.

Maria cuddled the little one and stroked the few dark curls on the crown of her head.

She looked up at Father Thomas Doyle.

"You must be so proud of this wonderful cathedral, Father. Everyone knows you were the one who raised the money to buy the site and build it. We can read the Notice Board," she blushed, "and *The Times* and *The Tablet*, if we are lucky enough to find a mucky old copy on the street."

"Someone described it as Father Doyle's Folly."

He offered the mother a tawny wicker shopping basket.

"There is a drop of Irish whiskey for the father, Jonathan, ale for the boys, lemonade for Rosa, and milk for the nursing mother."

He smiled down at her.

"I thought the pork pies and currant buns might be shared among the family to celebrate the birth of your lovely little one."

"You must be the kindest man in this world, Father."

Tears were streaming down her face.

"Tonight we shall have our first family party."

She knelt on the tiled floor and kissed his hand.

★★★

Father Doyle was a devout believer.

Many Catholic men and women living in the rookeries

haunted the confessional to reveal their sins: theft, murder, work as pimps and prostitutes. Cockfighting and bear-baiting. A few worked as mill hands, dockers and errand boys.

In his late twenties, Father Doyle had made a firm decision. Come what may he would raise the money to build a Catholic Church in Southwark, large enough to hold all the worshippers praying on the side-walk in the snow and sleet.

Nowadays devout Catholics knelt in the muck and mire.

He would talk to all his friends and beg around the world!

Europe was a shambles but there were still royal courts and kings.

His own diocese was poor but it lay close to a wealthy area over the water.

He would travel across Europe, France, Italy and Saxe-Coburg and approach the Catholic gentry, the Petres, the Earl of Shrewsbury and the Howards.

Somehow, by the grace of God…

★★★

In 1837 a circular letter states: "On Sundays crowds of people are compelled to kneel outside the chapel, exposed to the open air and to the scoffs of rude and insolent passers-by."

Father Doyle's plans often met with frowns and chilly repulse.

He begged all over Europe for money – to build a fine church in Southwark. There were donations from the Kings of Bavaria and Sardinia, the King of France and his wife Marie Amèlie, and the Empress of Austria and Leopold who became the King of the Belgians. The Queen of Spain and the Catholic aristocracy offered their help, even the waifs and strays of St Patrick's, Soho, gave their pennies.

Doyle wanted a plot of land, a triangle, opposite the

Bethlehem Hospital, but he was told by the Bridge House Estate that it was already sold. He bid for land on the opposite side of the road and they agreed to sell the site for £3,200.

It had a frontage of 500 feet on St George's Road and nearly 100 feet on the Lambeth and Westminster Roads.

The plan must be completed within six years. Work commenced on 8th September 1840. A local architect drew up plans, but the Earl of Shrewsbury suggested Pugin and his design was chosen in 1839.

"The civic villas, witty Smith, have fled
As well as wood landscape,
Where once the water lilies bloomed
Are planted rows of brokers' shops."

Father wrote to Lucas, the Editor of *The Tablet*. He was trying to raise money for St George's Church.

"I received £20 from Henry this week and 20 from Peter the week before, and £25 I am to receive from Marmaduke next week or the week after, for St George's Church. I have lots of pearls and things of that sort, but the £5 notes please me more."

Pugin the Gothic architect, became involved in furniture design, vestments, stained glass, metal-work and embroidery. He worked on several cathedrals, usually Catholic, and some great halls including Adare Manor and Lurra Castle with his partner J.C. Grace.

Pugin may have been overwhelmed by this project. He submitted designs that were far too financially ambitious to be considered.

The main enquiries by the Committee were the cost and time involved in the project.

Pugin did not reply to the relevant questions at a meeting.

He collected his plans, took up his hat, wished the gentlemen Good Day, and walked away, out of the house.

Everyone was amazed by his behaviour.

"Common sense should have taught the Committee not to put such absurd questions to me. If you appreciate my design, adopt it, and carry out all or part, in its integrity or the means that are forthcoming."

He wrote to Dr Doyle on the 20th February 1839.

"I have a letter of yours which says £18,000 must complete the building. Subsequently you said you must have a church for £8,000; I then replied that the size of the church must be reduced."

Estimates were requested once again by a different Committee and Pugin sent another design. This time it was agreed that £20,000 was not to be exceeded.

The building site near Lambeth Palace had been agreed and work on the foundations began in September 1840.

Someone wrote of the Father's correspondence in *The Tablet*: "The letters of Father Thomas of St George's have been read and relished by Catholics all the world over. Full of wisdom and pathos, remarkable for the genial humour which is as natural to the Irish character as the shamrock to the soil."

Father Doyle wrote about Pugin: "No man in England appreciates Pugin more than Father Thomas, but he is as wild, is Welby Pugin, as the wild wind that sweeps over the cliffs of Pegwell; and, with all his whirlwinds and storms, Father Thomas fears him nought."

Recently Pugin had published a book – *An Earnest Appeal on the Establishment of the Hierarchy* – and it had been attacked by many. Father Doyle wrote: "One man is not great at everything and only a prudent, wise and steady, humble and quiet mind is fitted for such subjects as you roughly and unskilfully handle. Be wise unto sobriety."

Pugin was the first man to marry in St George's Cathedral; it was his third wedding.

She became a devoted wife, who shared his love of art and entered into his work projects, while watching over his now broken health with unfailing tenderness.

Pugin's designs were complete in 1839. There was sufficient space to house three or four servants to care for the priests. The large school would encompass 300 boys and 200 girls. The church should hold 2,500 worshippers. The house could accommodate four clergy.

Pugin appears to have been a brilliant but temperamental gentleman. Born in 1812, he achieved a fine reputation in his career when he was a very young man.

Augustus Welby Northmore Pugin helped to design the new Houses of Parliament in Westminster after the fire. Fire engines entered the buildings and shot water at the hammerbeam roof. Three regiments of guards and a detachment of cavalry were brought in to help. The Houses of Parliament caught fire in 1834 and ruined a great deal of the Commons, the Lords and St Stephen's Church. Workmen had used wooden tallies.

Pugin also worked on the Roman Catholic Church, Farm Street, Berkeley Square.

His loving wife was devastated when he died in 1852.

The whole future of St George's Church was to be affected by an official statement in October 1850.

Cardinal Wiseman, on his return to England as the first Archbishop of Westminster, would also find the time to spend in the diocese of Southwark, and he would make St George's Church his cathedral. He was known as administrator of Southwark. The Pope had the audacity to name an individual here and another as a bishop.

One day the Cardinal was hooted and stones were thrown at his carriage.

On the 6th December 1850 the Cardinal took possession of the church, crowded by nearly 150 priests. There was a sympathetic report in the *London News*:

"At length the Cardinal himself appeared, wearing a gorgeous mitre and pallium. Lastly came the Very Rev. Dr Doyle robed in the usual sacrificial garments."

The Cardinal wrote in a letter to Mgr Talbot – "The take was £94. I had received continual warning that I should be attacked and shot that day, but of course I despised all that."

The effigy of the Pope and also that of the Cardinal had been burned in all parts of England, especially London.

Father Doyle talks of the "evening dew", a lovely depiction of the booze. On Guy Fawkes Day he writes, "Near to our quiet Priest's House is the Metropolitan Emporium for 'fireworks'. Three shops of this kind have been making a rich harvest in days, and what with their flags and bands of music, and screaming crowds of little boys, we have a lively day of it. Sufficient rockets, Roman candles, and crackers have been sold since the morning to blow up a city."

Rosa's Pussy And Le Vicomte

Rosa was wandering along the alleyway, searching for any lost coppers that might be lying in the gutter. The little one nearly tripped over a fluffy black pussycat on the cobblestones, whose eyes were glazed and almost closed. Was it leaving this world or having a kip?

The little girl stroked its ears and tummy but the animal lay deathly still in her arms.

She could only hear a low purr.

The back door of a nearby house was wide open. Rosa cuddled her black baby, ran across the alley and knocked.

One of the servants might be kind enough to give her an old blanket and some stale fish from their bin. She felt the pussy's bare bones; it must be starving hungry. Sharp little teeth nipped her fingertips.

A low voice with a French accent called out, *"Viens ici, n'importe qui."*

Rosa walked into the drawing-room where a dark, serpentine man lay on a chaise longue covered in green velvet, with a copy of Lord Byron's *Don Juan* beside him on a low mahogany table.

"Comment ça va, ma petite?"

"I'm sorry to wake you up, Sir. I was looking for someone to feed this pussycat. She was lying stone-cold, on the cobblestones, and I think she might be dying."

"Do not worry, little one. My manservant, my valet

15

Marcel, will take great care of her. We will bring her back to life. Marcel!"

The young man had been waiting in the passageway for orders. He collected the little animal and swept out of the room.

The gentleman eyed the little girl.

"What is your name, chèrie?"

"Rosa. Rosa Kelly, Sir."

"I am known as Le Vicomte de Southwark. I shall call you Rosamunde. Do you speak French?"

"No. Mummy has taught me a little Irish – Erse, from the Gaelic."

The man's eyes were like slits.

"You brought me a little black pussycat, they are said to be lucky. Will you be my own pussy, a Tabby or a Persian?"

He leaned forward and stroked her long blonde hair. "Perhaps you are a Marmalade cat?"

There was a long pause. "Shall we play games together?"

"Oh yes, please Sir. That would be great fun."

Le Vicomte called his servant again.

"Fetch my ebony cane decorated with the gold crest. It lies next to the bed."

Marcel disappeared upstairs and the man whispered "I will tell you a secret, my love. I am a paedophile."

"I don't understand the word."

"I will teach you, darling."

Marcel had brought the weapon.

"Kneel on the footstool beside me and pull down your knickers, little one."

"That's a funny idea." Rosa was intrigued, so she obeyed the strange man.

Her soft bum rose in the air and the little girl giggled "I'm saying my prayers."

Le Vicomte gazed at the cleft in her arse and dreamed of anal sex but it was far too soon. She might scream the place down. He must try to be restrained for a while.

"You have a few hairs on your bottom; they are the colour of golden honey."

Le Vicomte slapped Rosa's bum, very, very gently, with his ebony cane. She squeaked, "I haven't been naughty!" She giggled.

It was all rather fun playing games with this stranger who looked like a giant salamander.

He licked her bum and kissed it better; a drop of blood oozed on to the carpet.

The child was silent for a few moments. The man asked "Do you want to look at my lower body?"

Rosa squeaked in amazement. "No, thank you, Sir. I've seen Daddy's when he wees in the privy pail and it's not a pretty sight. We all live together in one little room and I sleep on the floor."

"Years ago I had a lovely little pussycat called Ermyntrude. She fell out of my bedroom window, but landed on her paws. Someone told me they rotate in mid-air and land safely. I will take great care of your little black baby if that would please you."

"Thank you so much."

"I have two dogs living with me. One is a golden retriever, the other a bull mastiff. Visit me and play with them any time you are free from school. I suppose you go to St Patrick's or the Poor School?"

"St Patrick's. Father Doyle has been very kind to our family. We are poverty-stricken."

"I might be able to help you, in many ways."

He stroked the little girl's hands gently, from wrist to fingertips.

"Do you have any brothers or sisters, *ma petite*, or are you an only child, like me?"

"I have two brothers, Daniel and Felix, and a baby sister Lucia."

"I would love to meet them."

"Bye bye, Sir. I am going home now; Mummy will think I have lost my way or got into trouble."

Le Vicomte gave her two pennies from his brocade handbag.

"Come and see me again, sweetheart, and we will play more games. I will give you three pennies next time. We might suck lollipops together."

"I must tell my Papa about you."

"Sssch, Rosa. This is our secret, my little love. *Au revoir, Chèrie. Á demain.*"

"That pussycat might come back and lick my bum. It tickles now, like fleas or bugs."

"Don't worry, *ma petite*. People play these games in many of the Paris music halls. I went there with my mother when I was a little boy. She always told me fairy stories at bedtime. It is a long while ago, but I remember it well. Every night she went out on the town with her friends, but she tucked me up and said I was the love of her life.

"Years later I became a student at the Sorbonne, but I have never used my mental assets. My darling Rosamunde. *Munde* is the mouth in Germany. Rosy mouth. Lick your lollipops, little one. *Au revoir, Chèrie. Á demain.*"

Rosa waved goodbye from the doorway and gave him a naughty wink.

The pussycat had a full tummy. She crept back into the living-room and fell asleep in front of the blazing log fire.

Pictures of famous men and women hung on the tall oak-panelled walls of Le Vicomte's living-room: poets, artists and performers. There was a profile of the Emperor Suetonius who was always remembered for saying: "Women are for babies, boys are for pleasure."

A pale blue vase stood on the mantelpiece, encircled by a wreath of ivy leaves. It contained his mother's ashes, yet he loathed the idea of cremation. It was like Jeanne d'Arc, burned at the stake after the Inquisition.

A cut glass bowl full of dark purple lavender scented the air.

The master, Vicomte Alexandre, stroked his ebony cane and smiled. He called his manservant. "Marcel, a glass of bubbly, then you may put me to bed. I need an early night. Tomorrow there will be a cock-fighting party at the George Inn. The boys must rub the silver spurs on my roosters, Sodom and Gomorrah and Castor and Pollux. I will lay my bets in the morning. Tell one of the men to polish the red leather on my cockfighting chair." He raised his glass. "I have a new little friend. *Santé,* Rosa. *Salut.*"

Rosa danced in the alley clutching her pennies. She was late for her stale bread and dripping at tea-time, it would be rock hard. She banged on the broken door. "I'm hungry, but I've had a glass of lemonade. Mummy, Mummy, guess what I've got."

Her face was as flushed as a baby beetroot.

"I met this great big man with a black beard and green slitty eyes. He grabbed me by the hair and pushed me down beside him. Then he gave me tuppence."

Jonathan said, "Oh my God, did he hurt you? I will kill the bugger."

"He only pulled down my breeches and slapped my bum. Then he kissed it better and said 'Bye bye, Little One'."

She thrust her paws under Mummy's nose.

"It's a lovely way to make a living."

She threw her two pennies on to the floor and giggled. "I'm going back again."

A few drops of blood seeped down her legs. Daddy Jonathan was listening to her story.

"Not on your bloody Nellie, child. My daughters are not child prostitutes working in whorehouses for dirty old men."

Maria laughed. "Lucia is a bit young to go on the game."

Rosa piped up. "The man told me a secret, Daddy, but I can tell you. He is a Paddy-Filly. I suppose that means a little Irish mare, but it doesn't make sense to me."

"Paddy is Irish and a filly is a young lady horse," Jonathan said.

"Someone should report the filthy bugger to the Metropolitan Police. I would do it myself but I could not prove anything with only two pennies as my evidence. I know the bastard would lie his head off."

★★★

Le Vicomte's manservant knew where the Kelly family lived. He had seen Rosa dancing in and out of the cabin door.

His master decided to send the little girl a present and an invitation to tea and games. There was a picture of a fluffy black cat on the card. The gift was a bag of lollipops and a blue silk scarf decorated with flowers.

Rosa's parents were firm.

"We would not dream of allowing you to visit that dirty old man again. Not for all the tea in China. He's got the morals of a wild animal and he doesn't give a damn about anyone but himself."

"The scarf is so pretty, Daddy."

"Keep it if you must. It will look great with your old torn trousers."

Jonathan filched a page of letter paper from St Patrick's School and wrote a firm but polite note to Le Vicomte.

"I regret to say that my daughter will never be free to visit you again. Please do not attempt to arrange this. Father Doyle might be able to assist you in the confessional with some of your problems."

Le Vicomte de Southwark was in a furious temper on receipt of this letter. Now he would never have his way with Rosa. As the Cockneys often said "'E fancied 'er rotten."

The valet was delighted not to be involved in this skulduggery, but, oddly enough he was still fond of his lord and master.

The little black pussy-cat gobbled up a pile of stale fish and was sick on the kitchen floor. "The moggy is still with us, milor'. She did not follow the little girl down the alleyway."

Le Vicomte nicknamed her Madeleine, remembering the naughty girl in the Bible stories.

"Perhaps she is looking for a tom-cat to satisfy her sexual urge? You might find her a mate in the stables of the George," he mused. "I wonder whether there were cats on the Isle of Lesbos? I know Sappho wrote passionate poems that excited her female coterie. I have heard tell of a slate-blue Chartreuse breed. They seem to be very rare. Find me one."

A while later Marcel asked his master, "Have you met Father Doyle, milor'? They say he is a very understanding priest. He might be able to solve some of your problems, milor'."

"How dare you suggest such a thing, Marcel? Lord Byron and I have tried to lead the good life, in our own way. English readers think he is angelic – the bloody fools."

A young man found the pathetic stray cat, Madeleine, asleep on his windowsill and he adopted her. His paintings might give her immortality, hanging in the Academy not on the gallows.

The cat never became a lesbian but gave birth to three little kittens.

Thank God, she would not be skinned and eaten by a poverty-stricken costermonger.

The following evening Le Vicomte Alexandre chose oysters and caviar to be part of his high tea.

"They are aphrodisiacs," he said. "The birds have eaten their maggots; the kitchen boys chopped them. I wish to lay a bet on my own four cocks. I am sure one of them will win, then I shall have a pound in pennies for my future entertainment. I could have worn fancy dress for this party, harlequin or Pierrot. I might have put charcoal on my nose, pretending to be one of the roosters."

Many noisy commoners were watching from the gallery in the tavern. He could hear the brogue and the Cockney accent.

"The bog Irish seem to breed like bunny rabbits. Bugger that for a lark. It's not my scene to encourage little bastards into this world. I was born out of wedlock. Leave me now, Marcel. I have seen a very attractive young man at the bar. Ask him to join me on this leather settee. The pub seems to be very short of chairs."

The boy was young and naïve; he accepted the offer.

"Thank you, Sir."

"The cocks keep me company when I travel alone."

"This seems to be a cruel sport."

"None of us will live for ever. I shall be happy to go when the time comes."

Le Vicomte drank from his glass of bubbly.

Stanislaus O'Hara stood at the bar of the George Inn enjoying his one and only indulgence of the day – a glass of pale ale and a chunk of cheddar cheese.

He had been working hard in his little shop, Fur and Feathers, creating mink stoles, bonnets and hats decorated with ostrich feathers for the gentry. The height of fashion.

He enjoyed any creativity.

A tall, slim man beckoned him from a leather sofa nearby saying, "Do come and join me, Monsieur. The bar is very crowded tonight. You are more than welcome."

"Thank you, Sir. It has been a hard day; I shall be happy to sit down for a while."

The French man laughed. "'Park your bum', as I believe they say in English. I am here to watch the cock-fighting, among other things. Two of my roosters are known as Castor and Pollux. I am sure you have watched it all before. My cocks wear silver spurs. They begin to fight when they are two years old, and boost their diet with steak, brandy and urine."

Stanislaus said, "It sounds disgusting to me. I love animals, this is not my scene."

Le Vicomte laid his tapering fingers, gently, on the young man's arm.

"I will lay bets for both of us and choose an outsider as well as my own birds."

He ferreted in his jacket pocket.

"Would you like a pinch of snuff?"

He offered the boy a beautiful azure enamel box by Fabergé.

"What is your name, young man?"

"Stanislaus, Stanislaus O'Hara."

"I am nicknamed Le Vicomte – Le Vicomte de Southwark. When the cock-fighting is over we could go upstairs to my suite and share a bottle of bubbly, and maybe absinthe, the drug known as the green fairy."

"I can't bear to sit here and watch these poor birds die. I think I will say goodbye now, Monsieur."

Le Vicomte whispered, "You might have been my favourite courtesan. A lady friend of mine adored animals, and sex with big dogs. She gave birth to three puppies, half-animal and half – human – French poodles. The doctor put them all to sleep. It was so sad, I would have cherished them."

Stanislaus was beginning to feel sick. He had never slept with a whore or a virgin, man or beast – or a "French Poodle".

Stanislaus had wanted to draw the cocks. A cartoon of their beaks, like the nose of this strange man beside him.

A quarter of an hour passed. The roosters might be drunk on their diet of brandy and urine, steak and maggots. One fell to the ground, squawked, and was silent. The handler strode on to the ring and waved the bird's body in the air. The neck was pierced by a silver spur.

The birds had been pecking at the beaks and throats of their opponents. "Do they have a brain, like human beings? Is it violently aggressive?"

The boy wanted to spew into the ring.

He shuddered. "I think this game is sad and cruel. I'm going home."

"Stay with me a while longer, my valet will collect any betting money."

"You can throw it into the ring, Sir. I don't give a damn."

"Have you heard of the Marquis de Sade? He went to prison for his ideas, but some of them were fascinating, like the loves of the late Lord Byron."

"I am leaving you now, Monsieur. I have no idea of your real name."

The serpentine man chuckled, a deep throaty sound.

"A Count of no account. I dare not involve my family in some of my escapades. In England they call me Le Vicomte de Southwark." Once again he took the young man's hand in his long, white tapering fingers.

"Change your mind. Come upstairs with me for glasses of bubbly and *eau-de-vie?* The water of life. We could play games for an hour or two."

"No, thank you, Monsieur Le Vicomte de Southwark. I read a book by the Marquis de Sade. It made me feel sick! I threw it away, drowned it in the river."

★★★

Stanislaus strode back to his little shop. Fur and Feathers was a studio with a bed at the rear. He felt starving hungry, opened the larder door and saw a giant rat. It disappeared swiftly down the back of the cupboard after scoffing the young man's supper of cheese and pork pie.

An easel holding a blank canvas stood near the back window.

There was a loud rap on the door and a woman emerged from the twilight.

"Good evening, Sir. I saw you come home. I have made a large bowl of vegetable soup. May I share it with you, Sir?"

"How kind! Come in, Madame."

They sat together at a low table, relishing their supper.

"I am one of the Irish tinkers living in a caravan by the riverside; I have been watching over you for quite a long while."

Now they were munching sultana buns from a little black knapsack she balanced on one plump hip.

A mouse scuttled across the floor, picking up crumbs. The crone laughed.

"I have gazed through your back window and watched you paint many animals, chameleons, birds and snakes. Pigeons, black birds and ostriches, many from your imagination. I could never kill an animal. How do you acquire stock for your shop and the studio?"

"You could be right to query it, Madame. Perhaps I should create a small art gallery instead of my Fur and Feathers."

"Bless you, Sir. One day I know you will be famous. The Wedgwood factory will soon need designs for their blue and white pottery. This could provide a small immediate income."

The tinker lady collected all her dirty crockery and packed it in her bag.

"I shall wash up in the caravan. I am living alone now. Good night, Sir. Sleep well and many thanks for your welcome. I will visit you again in the near future."

She paused in the doorway.

"You know I am a tinker, Sir. Our family came from Roumania to Youghal, in Southern Ireland, many years ago. I can tell your fortune without holding your hand and gazing at the palm. You will be a very lucky and successful man. There is a new style of painting and you will rise to the top of the hill. You might become a designer for the Doulton Pottery in Lambeth, or you could become another Leonardo da Vinci. God bless you, my boy, I wish you well."

The tinker lady continued, "Many of the English think the stories of Irish magic, superstition and fairies are crazy imagination. 'Kiss the Blarney Stone near Cork and you will have the gift of the gab for ever.' Be endowed with eloquence! The danger is hanging by one's feet from a castle, built in the fifteenth century. I think one must be very brave to dangle in mid-air; it would be so easy to fall to the ground, head first. I would rather be tongue-tied."

Stanislaus laughed. "I don't think that is a danger, Madame," and the old tinker carried on. She loved to find a listener, but that was not easy living alone in a caravan by the Thames.

"There are so many stories about plants and flowers, the four-leaf clover and the shamrock. The King of the

Leprechauns lives on the hills of Kerry and gives orders waving his shillelagh in the air. Irish folklore tells us the Irish leprechauns look like old men and they have buried treasure. They are able to find even more, hidden underground.

"Clover helps in the rotation of crops, but I have never seen any lucky ones with four leaves. Everyone knows the shamrock is the emblem of Ireland. They say it is a sign of death if anyone picks up a single flower from the ground."

Stanislaus said, "I have never heard that story before, but I think it may be true."

"It is past my bedtime, good night, young Sir."

Stanislaus had created his bedroom and studio at the back of the shop. He was surrounded by the tools of his trade: paints, brushes and an easel he had rescued from a garbage can. Models offered their services for coppers but Stanislaus chose animals. Stray cats and dogs, parrots and canaries, would serve him better than the girls from tarts' alleyways.

He had no wish to paint graffiti on the walls of whorehouses to advertise their assets!

The young man was a loner.

He stripped off, put on his nightshirt and lay down on the straw mattress, ruminating. The tinker crone had given him food for thought. How on earth could he say he loved animals and spend his working life selling their skins? Fur and Feathers.

The pelt of a little brown pony lay on his floor as a doormat. He remembered going to the zoo with his mother, father and sisters, Angelina and Teresa, and recalled the long necks of the giraffes and ostriches. Fur and Feathers! Animals were killed so he could adorn society ladies and make a profit from their bodies. Ostrich feathers became bonnets and handbags. Minks were capes and stoles.

Stanislaus had an idea, prompted by his little friend, the tinker lady. He would sell all the stock on a stall at the weekly market. Then he could design and decorate with paints and canvas, "pot and porc". Blue and white Wedgwood, little jugs and vases. Maybe he would offer examples of his own work, pictures of animals, snakes and rats and mice. Another world for Stanislaus O'Hara.

Oscar Wilde called it "Art for Art's Sake."

He remembered an ostrich in action in the gardens of the zoo. He got out of bed and picked up a leather-bound book. It might send him to sleep.

"The ostrich is a flightless bird. The males have short black body feathers and long white rump and wing feathers. Those of the female are dusty grey. In Africa they live in the wild. Minks are bred in minkeries and they stink."

A lynx jacket cuddled a silver fox fur in his shop window.

Stanislaus dropped the book and fell asleep dreaming of a new life.

★★★

It was late afternoon on a warm summer's day. School was over for the weekend, but there would be religion with a capital R on Sunday at St George's.

Rosa thought it might be fun to call on the old French gentleman and play games for coppers, but she dare not risk it, there would be a riot in the family. She did not really fancy the idea of him kissing and slapping her bum.

She trotted home for the usual dreary tea; stale bread and cheese, all as hard as nails. She might write a story and pretend it was English homework.

Prancing along, Rosa glanced down at the cobblestones and something lovely caught her eye. She bent down and grabbed it. Little Rosa danced down the alley waving a hand in the air; there was a flash of blood red in her pink paw.

Maria was sitting in the yard sewing patchwork with scraps of old material from the litter bins. She might be able to create a skirt or a shawl to keep out the wind.

Her long curly hair was tied back with a strand of old velvet ribbon from her wicker work-box. Her hands were as rough as sawdust from all the household tasks.

"Have you cut yourself, Rosa? I will cover it with an old bandage I washed this morning."

Rosa shook her head. "I have brought you a surprise, Mummy. A lovely red rose. I found it lying in the gutter near the cathedral."

"Oh, my God! Throw it down the drain, darling. Now. Now. I can't bear to touch it."

The child stammered, "I don't understand. What is wrong, Mummy?"

"Have you forgotten the old Irish superstition, little one? Pick up a flower from the earth and someone you know will die. I saw it happen when we lived in Ireland. I know he was an old man but he died the day he picked up a flower from the gutter."

Rosa was sick to death of taking orders from grown-ups.

She hid the lovely red rose in a mug of water under the broken pottery sink.

The perfume was far sweeter than wee-wee in the privy pail and the stinking sewage from the Thames.

One day Jonathan said, "Many people are dying of the cholera again. They say the worst epidemic here was in 1832, thank God we were still in Ireland at the time."

The rose fell on to the crumbling bricks and floated across the rotten floorboards.

Maria saw the sere brown petals.

"You are a little sod, my darling. I told you to throw the flower away. Now it is back to haunt us."

Maria fingered her rosary and whispered, "Ave Maria. Hail Mary, full of Grace. Blessed art thou among women and blessed is the fruit of thy womb, Jesus."

Southwark Fair to celebrate the Virgin was an orgy for pimps and prostitutes. It was fast becoming the only sure way to make a living.

Many women carried a bottle of animal blood. It was said to cure tuberculosis, but men preferred a drop of whiskey in their "nice cup of tea".

★★★

Felix liked working as a call boy at the South London Palace of Varieties. It gave him an excuse to peer into the dressing rooms, watch the stars mask their faces with grease-paint and "get in drag". He knocked on the doors saying, "You are on next, Sir. Five minutes to go."

Many artists were homosexual and fancied the pretty young boy, but restrained themselves from making a pass at him. It might have created adverse publicity.

When they were on stage Felix was able to gawp into their wardrobes and make-up bags.

Sometimes a performer might stagger on stage as drunk as a fart.

Felix was learning all the time and longed to make an entrance on stage. Somewhere? Anywhere. One day, maybe? It was a wild dream.

He watched a brilliant juggler and tried to copy him, but broke three wine glasses. It was not his scene.

Magicians, a ventriloquist working an act with a toy bunny rabbit. Three acrobats had escaped from a foreign circus.

A primitive escapologist freed himself from handcuffs and chains.

Two young men in drag worked a naff act with a couple of ponies who misbehaved on stage.

Felix cleaned up the muck and ran errands to the bar for tankards of plonk.

He was learning all the time, but missed out on sophisticated dates at the Garrick Club.

He saw the pros' antics in the Green Room of the theatre where they nattered together.

"Why do they call it the Green Room?"

"There is a very simple answer. They are nearly always painted green. Heaven knows why."

Some men wobbled in mid-air looking as though they might dive from a tight-rope or a trapeze. They always seemed to retrieve their balance after scaring the daylights out of the audience. Felix thought he would rather busk on the streets. His great ambition was to be a "song and dance man".

He was always willing to work back-stage after the show and often sang his heart out tidying the dressing-rooms.

Felix was learning something fresh about the theatre every day of his life.

He did not really give a damn about Reading, 'Riting and 'Rithmetic, although he was still a pupil at school.

These days bill-toppers were often pretending to be upper-class toffs.

Swell performers were tarted up in spats, monocles, garish suits, even Dundreary whiskers. These were known as Piccadilly Weeps, with sideburns, often a foot long.

The London Pavilion on the Haymarket was built in 1859 and by 1875 London had thirty music halls.

Good newspaper reviews could be an enormous help.

In 1856, *The Era* claimed to be the biggest newspaper in the world, and it catered for licensed victuallers.

Other papers and magazines were *The Tablet, The Magnet, The Entr'acte* and *The Encore*. Many fine artists used music hall performers as models: Sickert, Toulouse-Lautrec, Degas and Manet.

Manet's painting of *Le Déjeuner Sur l'Herbe*, with a naked woman lying on the grass, did not appeal to Stanislaus O'Hara.

He preferred Van Gogh's *Sunflowers* and admired the Impressionists.

Felix was wearing torn red knickerbockers; they glowed in the artificial light of the candles and oil lamps in the pub. His mother had tried to darn them with her only thread, black cotton. He was hiding under the bar counter hoping to watch a cabaret for the first time. Half-starved, yet he grew livelier every day. If any rooks or crows caught sight of his stale bread and dripping they swooped down to steal it. Cawing.

★★★

It was Saturday night and the roosters were released from their cages. Were they pissed on their diet of brandy and urine?

"Pit!" They attacked one another; a giant bird was the odds-on favourite.

The poverty-stricken costermongers and the bookies hoped to make a bomb.

Le Vicomte straddled his cock-fighting chair and felt the smooth red leather stroking him.

He was excited by his own birds in the ring and called out, *"Bonne chance, mes petits."*

The poor little ones had lost their wattles, sliced off by the handlers. Two survived after piercing their enemies with their silver spurs, a luxury gift from Le Vicomte.

He laughed, saying to his manservant, "Now I am rich enough to buy a boy or girl, or a babe. Thank God, tiny little animals have never been my scene. They might bite me where it hurts."

★★★

One night Stanislaus was thinking about his encounter with the French man. It was the first time any male had tried to seduce him. Girls might wiggle their hips and try to look enchanting, but all their efforts failed. Who knows? He might be asexual. He had read medical books about people who were heterosexual or homosexual. To Hell with all that codswallop!

He took a deep breath and sank into his one and only low armchair. He fancied a break from his work routine. A glass of ale and a sarnie, then he might feel energetic enough to work on his oil painting of a wolfhound.

Something nudged his elbow. Madeleine had jumped on to his lap baring her front teeth in a grin. Now she kissed him fondly on the cheek, there was a delicious smell about the man. (His sandwich was smoked salmon.)

She snuggled between his legs, coiled herself and lay still for a while. She stroked his hand with her whiskers and gave him another kiss.

The poor little animal might be hungry. He would provide three meals a day with sardines as a special treat. She was a lovely little creature.

Stanislaus fell asleep for half an hour and when he woke the lovely Madeleine had disappeared.

★★★

Le Vicomte said to Marcel, "You are a poor but educated boy. I suppose you admire the flamboyant Romantic poet, Lord Byron?"

The young man nodded.

"His love life was very strange; many say, tongue in cheek, that he was bisexual. One of his many mistresses, Lady Caroline Lamb, said, 'He is mad, bad, and dangerous to know.'

"There were so many love affairs with boys and girls, ladies and their maidservants. After fighting with one he spent the night on a gondola. He asked her to leave the house in Venice and she threw herself into the canal."

★★★

Daddy Jonathan said, "We can only live one day at a time. Only God knows what will happen tomorrow."

Rosa was longing to dance like Felix but she had two left feet.

Jonathan said, "It's all in the mind, but not the behind."

Sometimes he joined a few Irish men in a pub and they drank a toast to a saint, or a newborn babe.

The youngest Kelly, Lucia, was as bright as a button.

Felix was called The Happy One; his name in Latin meant happy and fortunate.

One of the school teachers told Felix, "You are a clever kid."

The boy laughed when he repeated the compliment to his father.

"I though a kid was a young goat, I suppose it's English slang."

He was learning about his favourite subjects, history, the theatre and life in Ireland, and borrowed many books from the new library. Father Doyle gave him a few coppers to pay.

"You know they changed the name of the Alhambra Theatre to the Panopticon? I looked that up and it means an assembly, showing every aspect in one view."

Jonathan replied, "I don't give a damn. I have never heard the word before."

"I think it is a bit would-be. I know *Alhambra* is the Spanish word for palace."

Jonathan was at a loose end. He wandered into the market at Covent Garden. This time he was alone.

A man was selling moustache grease on the street. He looked at the stubble on Jonathan's chin and grinned. "Some of the girls use it down below, if the boys prefer their bums to their faces."

Jonathan shuddered. "Piss off, boy. I don't want to know. The idea makes me sick."

★★★

One of the music hall stars at the South London Palace of Varieties fancied Felix, the pretty young call boy.

"Would you like to join me for supper in my dressing-room? I'm sure I could offer you something exciting. Crabs, prawns, lobsters? I know you are Irish, so we could share a few drops of 'the black stuff'."

"Thank you, Sir, but I must say 'No thanks'. My father will pick me up every night after the show. He only works in the day-time, in the stables of the George Inn, so he is free every night. You know they have cockfighting and bear-baiting at the pub. I think it is a horrible idea."

"I quite enjoy a little violence, when I am not involved."

A bidet lay in a corner of the dressing-room.

"Is that a foot-bath, Sir?"

"No, young man. It is something a little more intimate.

One hotel near the Boulevard Haussmann in Paris has five bidets in the bathroom of a double bedroom. I think that is a little excessive." The star said, "Well, Felix, I am sad we must say goodbye – unless you want me to demonstrate the bidet?"

"No, thank you Sir." Felix fled the coop.

A few years later Felix was told the star performed at orgies on the Paris Left Bank, Le Rive Gauche.

Father Doyle said to Felix, "We all know the theatre is a dangerous profession for the young and innocent. You can always ask my advice if any problems arise."

Auguste, one of the back-stage staff at the Elephant and Castle Theatre, listened to Felix humming, whistling and singing in the wings.

"I think you might have a future in the theatre, boy. You could make a small fortune. I would like to be your manager. Do you have the guts to entertain a drunken crowd in the parks? They play from seven o'clock till midnight."

He laughed.

"I'm afraid your lessons at St Patrick's School might take a battering. You could be half-asleep the morning after a show, but what the Hell? I expect you have heard of the Gatti Brothers. They own the "Theatre Under the Arches". It's in the undercroft below the railway, under the Thames. They call some of their shows 'trying it out on the dog'. A lot of talented old and new pros work there. The artists perform on a high square platform, not a stage, to an audience of about 400 people. Young Rudyard Kipling lives nearby on Villiers Street. He spends a lot of time watching the shows and thinks some of them are great. He wrote 'My One and Only' for a Lion Comique at Gatti's."

Auguste warned the boy. "Of course, you might get cat-calls, boos, and rubbish thrown on to the stage. I'm not worried, are you?"

"No way. If you are willing to take a gamble on me I will have a go."

His new manager said, "I shall expect a whopping percentage."

Felix laughed, "You should be so lucky."

They shook hands on the deal. The boy's pipe dreams might come true.

Felix said to his new manager, Auguste, "For Pete's sake don't call me The Wonder Boy. I would blush like a beetroot. You know I have never walked on a stage before."

"I'm going to advertise your debut somehow. I know, I've got a far better idea and you won't say 'No' to this one. I shall call you The Golden Boy. We will buy you a gold lame scarf from one of the stalls on Covent Garden and drape it round your neck. Things like that are dirt cheap; you might go shopping with your dad."

"That sounds OK. As long as you haven't got some crazy idea of draping my bum in a golden tutu. I have seen some ballet dancers flashing their naked bodies under transparent lace."

"Don't worry; I haven't got any daft ideas like that. I really believe you might become a star in cabaret and the music halls, but it's bound to take a year or two. You are only a kid. Now, I suggest you work a three-minute act in one of the parks at night-time. How about that?"

"It sounds great. Give me a few days to organise everything."

The man laughed. "Perhaps you should warn your father, Felix, otherwise he might think I am leading you astray."

When Maria heard the latest news from the Elephant she said, "Be ready to weep. You might get the bird."

Did she mean caterwauling or applause?

"For God's sake be careful, darling. Some of the gentry are as queer as coots."

Father Jonathan laughed, saying "Don't worry. I will always pick him up at the end of a show."

Moonlight. Candleglow. A drunken audience roaring with laughter.

Felix danced across the boards for the first time in his life, shaking like a leaf. Stage fright. He had the jitters. Night had fallen.

Felix was dressed in his father's best clothes, but the trousers were far too big; he might lose them during the act. He had tied an old rope round his waist.

Jonathan called out, "Go for it, boy" and he sang his heart out and pranced around.

A man in the audience picked up the tune by ear and played it on his Irish hornpipe.

The youngster gave the audience a lopsided wink and a smile to fetch the ducks off the water. Two naughty street girls sitting in the front row fancied this young boy with the black curly hair and sparkling deep blue eyes. They began chirruping, fluttering their lips to offer their services to this fabulous young man for free.

One moment he was a swell, then he stripped to reveal the every-day clothes of a working man, breeches and a torn shirt. Now the girls were blowing kisses. One called out, "May I pull your rope?"

It had come undone and was dangling round his ankles. He might lose his pants?

Later the organiser said, "Your act went very well. You are on again tomorrow, Felix. Would you like a tankard of ale to celebrate?"

"I am a bit thirsty but I would rather have a mug of lemonade. I am only eleven years old, Sir."

"Some kids are pissed at five."

Jonathan loomed in the background.

"This is my dad. He would go bonkers if I hit the bottle."

The Old Chapel In The London Road

The chapel had served the parish for fifty-eight years, from 1790 to 1848. Father Doyle had made the grade at last and raised the money to build St George's.

In 1849 Dr Wiseman invited a community of nuns to take over the chapel. They embraced the offer and were known as the Benedictine Solitaries of the Perpetual Adoration.

The building became the Abbey of the Solicitous and Handmaids of Jesus and Mary.

Provost Doyle went away for his holidays and even more begging tours.

"I am growing old and lazy. I have been down to Hastings to get cool in that hot place, and to Paris and Normandy and Namur. Liverpool gave me the cold shoulder; Manchester I hate with all her cotton and all my heart, for all I caught there was the bronchitis."

He travelled to Spain and returned in February the following year.

Mock Orange Blossom

A little blond stable lad with sky-blue eyes was lurking behind the bar at the George Inn.

He was over the moon when Le Vicomte chose him as a companion.

His mother had been a harlot with a hand on the purse strings.

"Tomorrow we will go to the bear-baiting together."

"I have been there once already, Sir. It is scary. They have great big gates."

The following day the gentry and the costermongers trooped towards the bear garden. A poor old brown animal was dragged into the ring by an elderly Russian fellow. A chain was clamped to its jaw. The creature tottered on his hind legs, mangey, going bald with age and neglect.

Two snarling bulldogs attacked him and the crowd bellowed.

Blood poured from a torn leg.

At last the poor old beast roared, caught hold of one dog and flung him across the ring. He writhed then lay inert. The audience screamed.

Le Vicomte said, "The party's over. Come upstairs with me later and we will share a bottle of wine, a pinch of snuff, and maybe another little treat?"

Drink and drugs. Sex and senility.

"Thank you, my lord. I think we shall spend a lovely night together."

Booze and Bonhomie. Mock Orange Blossom

Later Le Vicomte asked, "Can you read and write, boy?"

The youngster shook his head.

"I escaped from the workhouse when I was nine years old. I never went to the Poor School, Sir, but I have been working for years, in and out of bed." He giggled, thinking this story might encourage the old French nobleman to offer him a few coppers. He was aware of money at twelve years of age.

"I saw you gazing at the book on my coffee table, *Don Juan* by Lord Byron."

"I know he was long before my time but I recognised his picture on the cover. I think my mother met him once at a party, when she was very, very young. I was born years and years later."

Le Vicomte said, "I think I would rather play games with little boys than little girls, but they are both fun. They say many children enjoy a wonderful time, it is a way of life they would choose."

"My two sisters are married and they think I am crazy, but I am happy and I earn a few coppers. I muck out the stables at the George Inn when they have cock-fighting."

Le Vicomte said, "That is a good name when you think about it."

There was a long pause while they gazed at one another. The boy lay on the carpet at the man's feet, stretched his arms and yawned.

"I think I shall christen you, little one. You will be my Goldilocks."

"I can remember a fairy story about *Goldilocks and the Three Bears*."

"I will buy you three brown toy animals and we could take them to bed with us every night."

"Oh yes, please Sir. That is a lovely idea."

★★★

In 1849 Father Doyle wrote, "If I were a very rich man I should think one mourning coach and ten feet of St George's tower (of my own building) would be better than a long, expensive funeral affair of nodding plumes and sable, of mourning coaches and mutes and staff-bearers, and legacies and rings and mementoes to those who would laugh and junket on my funeral day, and be glad I was gone and done with.

"What a waste of money is all this cavalcade and vain pomp over a mass of putrefaction. Opera and race course, *rouge et noir*, masquerades and bull fights.

"The evening before I attended a young woman from the land of sighs and tears, of working and of mourning – Ireland. She was the first I ever saw passing from life through starvation. Poor child, she had been picked up on the streets and taken to the workhouse. Her face was of that sweet, placid expression that wins one to compassion. The poor are thrust aside and driven away to starve and die. Bless the Lord."

★★★

Whenever Mother Maria was exhausted, Felix took his little sister Lucia out into the yard and they played drumming on rusty old saucepan lids with wooden spoons.

The noise terrified the stray cats and wild rabbits, but they had a great time.

The boy was longing to go back to Waterford and live in a wooden cabin near the harbour at Passage East.

In the olden days, before the famine, one might find fruit and vegetables on the strand.

Danny was the only one of the children who could remember their old life in Eire.

So many of the poor Irish could not afford to pay their rent on time.

One day the English mob arrived outside some cottages on the hill, demanding money for their masters. Every penny had been spent.

The Kellys and many others were ordered to collect their children, clothes and food.

Families stood at the side of the road and watched the servants of the English lordlings set fire to their homes. Orange and lemon flames lit the sky.

Tears flowed down Maria's cheeks. Danny bellowed like a cow, Jonathan was longing to shoot the bastards.

At dawn, Jonathan sold his shot gun and a tiny gold cross, a dying gift from his old mother.

The family paid a few pence to cross the harbour on the ferry, then walked for miles and sailed the Irish Sea.

One evening Felix said, "Will you take me to Covent Garden, Dad? I'll never find my way there alone."

"Why on earth do you want to go to that scruffy area?"

"Drury Lane, Dad. The Drury Lane Theatre. It's one of the oldest in London and someone said I might play there one day."

"Alright, boy. We will go and have a look, but the surroundings are awful."

Everything was on sale in Covent Garden Market, from watercress to winkles and pigs' feet. It stank. Buskers were performing and begging for pennies. Felix wondered if he would ever make it through the stage door.

Felix recited to his dad:

"Speak roughly to your little boy and beat him when he sneezes.

He only does it to annoy, because he knows it teases."

He grabbed his father's hand. " I'm going to buy you a little present for bringing me here. I know you think it's all a waste of time."

"You haven't any money, kid. Don't turn into a pick-pocket, for Heaven's sake."

"No way, Dad. Would you like a pork pie?"

An old crone had a food stall nearby, selling eels, oysters and stale lumps of cheese.

"May I use your empty seat for a few minutes, Madam?" The woman nodded and the boy jumped up on to the chair, flung his arms wide open and began to sing. "Auld Lang Syne – Come drink a cup of kindness yet for the sake of Auld Lang Syne."

An audience gathered round and one man threw three coppers at his feet. He called out, "I'm a Scot from Auld Reekie. You will go far, young man. Good Luck."

A shower of coppers was scattered in the air. Dad Jonathan stood open-mouthed.

"I learned about King Charles, Nell Gwynne and Drury Lane at school. Come on Dad, let's go shopping and buy everyone a surprise."

Father Doyle was delighted when the boy joined the choir at St George's while he played the organ.

Mavourneen

The show at the London Pavilion in the Haymarket was over after a standing ovation and many curtain calls. Felix Kelly sat in front of the mirror in his dressing-room and began to clean the grease-paint from his face. His dresser hung a dinner jacket on the door.

"You can go home now, boy. It's getting late and I'm old enough to cope by myself."

Alone at last, he sat daydreaming about the family.

Mum and Dad were happy, fighting like Kilkenny cats or making love on the tester bed in their pig sty.

Daniel and Teresa were Dubliners. Lucia might become a pupil at Cheltenham Ladies' College with the gentry, but he thought she would be out of her depth.

Felix was alone. Now, in his early twenties, he had been offered a short tour in the U.S.A. He was dithering. It might be a long, lonely journey for a bachelor, but it would be fantastic if he had the chance to appear on Broadway.

Felix peered at a tiny wrinkle on his forehead and saw a movement reflected in the mirror. The chintz curtain covering his wardrobe trembled. It might be a fan, a burglar or an assassin?

"Come out of there, you bugger."

He raised his hands in the air to slap down the intruder if he became aggressive.

His one and only toy bear, Alfie, popped his nose round

the corner. A pretty little girl followed him. She was wrapped in a pair of his theatre trousers to keep warm. Blonde hair. Peaches and cream.

"What on earth are you doing in there?"

"I'm so sorry, Sir. I never meant to frighten you."

Felix laughed. "I'm Irish. We are not easily scared."

She whispered, "I was four years old, riding on Daddy's shoulders, when I saw you perform in Dublin. You sang Irish ballads."

Felix recognised the accent. Thank God, this lovely little girl was neither an English aristo nor the scum of the earth. So many grew up in the gutter. Was she a shamrock or a four-leaf clover to bring him luck? She might have escaped from one of the workhouses where wives, husbands and children were segregated. Nearly everyone worked ten hours a day, six days a week, for their bed and board. According to the newspapers "30,000 children go to the workhouses every year".

The system could be horribly cruel, many were sent from the workhouses to the other side of the world. All these ideas were scudding through his mind. The girl was in danger, roaming the streets of theatreland; the Haymarket.

Felix had often seen young men playing games in the open air after a few bottles of wine. They stripped off their trousers and underpants and pranced around in a circle, holding left hands.

Someone would bring a basket of ostrich feathers. The youngsters danced, singing a little tune, and tickling one another up the bum.

"My name is Colleen. I've lost my daddy. He was fighting for a free Ireland, then it was time to escape. We were sailing to America on a coffin ship but I missed the boat and was stranded in this country. My darling mummy died years ago, I have lost touch with everyone."

"Don't worry darling, I will take care of you with the help of my dresser and his wife."

★★★

Daniel Kelly's tummy rumbled like a horse and cart travelling across the cobblestones. He farted.

The room stank with all the bodies asleep on the floor, and the wee-wee in the privy pail tucked away in a far corner of the room. He could smell the dirty laundry waiting to be washed in the morning. Piss and pooh!

It was freezing cold; Danny shivered and scrambled to his feet. Early evening, about seven or eight o'clock. He fancied a hot cup of tea but he would never find the odds and ends in the half-light.

He put his rusty old navy blue overcoat over his underpants and donned a battered tweed cap rescued from a litter bin. None of the males could afford a nightshirt or pyjamas.

Jonathan said, "We can't aspire to them, even second hand, but I am sure they are worn by some of the Royal family. I can imagine Queen Victoria and Prince Albert wearing posh clothes at bedtime. He laughed. "Maybe that is why Her Majesty has given birth to so many boys and girls."

Danny Kelly chose to walk by the Thames, it might make him sleepy.

The stink of sewage from the river was even worse than the pong in his own home. He set off at a good speed and began to warm up, but his toes and fingers were still ice-cold. He should have borrowed his father's old mitts and worn leather shoes.

It was early autumn. The boy shivered and tied his tattered scarf tighter round his neck.

A shadow crossed his path and Danny saw a lovely

young girl with a lurcher on a long leather lead. He could not get a clear view in the twilight but heard her talking to the doggy, with an Irish accent. "Come along, Paddy, you have done your business; now we are going home for tea. I know Angie has made you some fresh dog biscuits and a meat jelly."

Daniel had been intrigued by the dog, now he gazed at the young girl.

She caught sight of him for the first time in her life, smiled and said, "Good Evening."

He could see her dark Titian hair and a smile to bring the ducks off the water.

The girl tightened Paddy's long leash and walked away.

The next evening Danny waited almost half an hour to see the young girl walk her dog. She appeared at last; the boy was hiding in the shadows, he did not want to scare her.

A stray black cat ran across the alley-way and the lurcher broke his leather leash struggling to race after it.

The girl called, "Paddy, come back here," but he was chasing his prey and ignored her.

The poor kid tottered, lost her balance and fell backwards onto the cobblestones.

Danny ran forward to catch her but he was too late.

She hit the side of her forehead on a lump of wood and Paddy came drifting back and tried to lick it better.

"You naughty dog," and she fainted.

Danny lifted her body from the ground; she was as light as a feather. He would carry her back to the villa on Bandyleg Walk.

A tall dark man answered the door, glaring at the boy.

"What the Hell are you doing with my daughter Teresa?"

"She fell in the gutter trying to catch the dog. He followed her home, I couldn't leave her there."

Michael relented now he understood the problem, and was grateful.

"Bring her inside, boy, and we will lay her on the settee in the living-room. My other daughter, Angelina, will make us tea and bandage Teresa's forehead."

Paddy the lurcher lay on a rug nearby. Teresa had regained consciousness long ago and lay silent and inert. The pain in her head was horrible.

"Do sit down, young man.

I know, we will both cheat a little and have a drop of brandy in our cuppas."

The man spoke with a strong Dublin accent.

"Tell me about yourself. Are you still at school or working?"

"Neither one nor the other. I left the Poor School, but I can't find a job anywhere. My name's Daniel Kelly, we live in the slums near Glean Alley. My father, Jonathan, works part time in the stables of the George Inn. We can't pretend to be grand in any way."

"I'm Michael O'Hara, I'm a wharfinger on the Thames, carrying goods between Southwark and Richmond. Let's shake hands, boy. It's a godsend you found my daughter. She might have got into trouble, even been kidnapped by a pimp."

Teresa was listening to the conversation while pretending to be asleep.

A black baby grand piano stood by the drawing-room window.

"You might join us for a musical evening. Do you play or sing?"

"Only the Irish hornpipe, Sir. My brother Felix can sing and dance."

"How big is your family?"

"There are six of us altogether. I am the oldest child, then there is Felix and two sisters, Rosa and Lucia."

Michael's voice was soft. "I am a widower, my wife died of tuberculosis. We had three children, Stanislaus, Angelina and Teresa. Life can be lonely." There were tears in his eyes.

Michael O'Hara said to Danny, "I think you have certain private ambitions but are frustrated by lack of money. Will you work as a docker with me? I pay a fair wage. Perhaps our families were destined to meet, after all we share the same brogue."

Teresa lay motionless on the settee. She opened her eyes for a moment and saw this handsome young man holding her hand.

The lovely young girl turned towards Daniel and fell asleep.

★★★

When Father Doyle gave his lady worshippers three pence each after the service he was warned it might be wasted on a nip of gin, but that did not concern him.

One Sunday morning Angelina O'Hara approached Maria.

"We would love to meet all the Kellys. Will you come to us for an evening meal? We will keep it simple; there is no need to dress up."

That was a great relief; it would have been impossible!

"Our father often plays the grand piano and we have a sing-song."

Maria was delighted with the invitation and the two families had a great time together. There was even a little light entertainment from Felix, The Golden Boy.

Daniel and Teresa became closer every day.

Danny and Teresa had spent an evening together watching a

Shakespeare play, *Romeo and Juliet*, at the Globe Theatre on the Strand.

She trilled, "'What's in a name. A rose by any other name would smell as sweet'."

He escorted her home, then fell to one knee on the drawing-room carpet.

"I love you, Teresa. I shall always love you. Will you marry me?"

She touched his hand.

"Yes, Oh, yes. You must know it is my dearest wish. I have been longing for you to ask me."

Danny rose to his feet and kissed her gently on the lips.

"I think Juliet was twelve years old. You are seventeen. Shall we tell your father tonight?"

Michael O'Hara said, "I hope you live happily ever after, like the fairy stories. Thank the Lord the Kellys and the O'Haras are not deadly enemies, Montagues and Capulets. You know some of the Irish children learn Shakespeare in the hedge schools, hiding from the English soldiers. Schooling was forbidden for a while, and some of the teachers, the priests, were shot.

"Thank God we have Father Doyle, I am sure he will be happy to marry you himself.

I read *Hamlet* years ago.

'To be or not to be, that is the question.

Whether 'tis nobler in the mind to suffer the slings and arrows of outrageous fortune or to take arms against a sea of troubles and, by opposing, end them?'."

Michael coughed and wiped a tear from his eyes, remembering his dear wife.

"This should be a happy time for all of us."

He took a small emerald ring from his jacket pocket and gave it to Daniel.

"This was ours. Will you accept it as an engagement ring?"

Teresa said, "I shall always kiss my rings good night."

Teresa was plucking the petals from a pink rose by the garden gate.

"He loves me, he loves me not.

He would if he could but he can't.

He loves me …"

It might take Danny years to save enough from his wages as a docker to fulfil his dreams – marry Teresa, sail home to Ireland and raise a family.

She dried her eyes and knelt beside the bed to say her prayers.

Father Doyle said, "Believe, my child, and it will all come true."

Teresa would never forget the night she saw the balcony scene in Romeo and Juliet.

This was her dream: 'To love one man more than life itself.'

The Kellys were sitting in a circle on the floor of their broken-down hovel.

Lucia lay in the middle on Grandma's old woollen shawl.

Jonathan topped up the tankard of his wife's watery milk with a drop of the hard stuff. He had nicked it from the cellars of the George.

Lucia moaned, "This bread is foul."

Maria said, "I'm sorry love. I know some of the market traders make it with flour and chalk. I may have been unlucky."

"I think I shall be as sick as a pig." The child burped.

Danny was trying to make conversation but all the others were too tired to listen to his prattle.

"I always wanted to be a lighthouse keeper. I read a story

in school about a brave girl called Grace Darling. She rescued nine men from a sinking ship called the *Forfarshire.* The lighthouse-men were too cowardly to set off in the storm."

One of the family was snoring; it was time for the boy to shut up.

Danny blew out the four candles in the wicker basket. It was far too cold to undress unless the mother was chasing them.

Maria lolled against the bare wall with her head in Father's lap and snored.

The Kellys all slept like logs until the morning light streamed through a hole in the bare wall.

Once upon a time it had been a kitchen window.

Daddy Jonathan told his wife Maria "They say there are more than 400 pawn shops in London now, they must be making a packet. So many people can't afford to retrieve their possessions.

I saw a few odd things on my trip to Uncle's. There was one strange pub sign. An elephant with a howdah on its back."

"What on earth is a howdah? I've never heard the word before, it must be foreign."

"I looked it up in that old dictionary. A howdah was used by the gentry. It is a carriage with a canopy and railings, so they can't fall off the animal.

I saw a lot of errand boys in little black suits and small top hats. All very grand.

One organist with a wooden barrow had a real monkey dancing on top. There is even a Punch and Judy show on the street, but it only starts at 2pm.

Living in a rookery in Southwark we seem to be missing our on so many things.

Oh, there is something else I forgot to tell you.

There is gas lighting since the Prince Regent's coming of age."

"It all sounds fantastic. We must leave the kids and have a night out on the tiles."

Maria laughed. "Can I pawn you?"

Michael O'Hara said to Angelina, "I know the Kellys are penniless and I would love to help them. The trouble is Jonathan and Maria are too proud to accept charity. Danny talks about living in the rookeries, a name for hovels where black birds nest in the roof. The slums.

"I had an idea. I could give the little ones a penny or two, pocket money, every week. They might spend some of it on the market. Angelina, we might invite them to dinner once a week."

"You know I love cooking, Father. They could always take home any left-overs."

"I am sure they will be delicious, darling. Do not become too posh or you will cost me a fortune and the O'Haras will be forced to move into the slums."

Rosa licked her lips when she saw the chocolate dessert served with thick cream, and the little tarts with their cherries and sugar icing.

Their weekend treat had been four oysters for a penny.

One day the two families met by chance on the street.

There was a long pause.

"I know it's not very generous, Michael, but can I offer you a 'nice cup of tea'." She said it with a cod, theatrical Irish accent.

"Thank you, Maria, that would be great. I'm thirsty after walking by the river."

Jonathan came bouncing in on his lunch break from the pub.

They sat on empty wooden crates and cardboard boxes, swilling their cuppas.

Jonathan was delighted to see Michael. The man did not pretend to be one of the higher echelon, although he owned money and a house.

After a few minutes he broke the silence.

"I suppose you realise that Danny and Teresa have become very close?"

"I have overheard them talking about love and marriage."

"My father is on his last legs with prostate cancer. He knows I want to stay in England for the time being so he has left his Dublin cottage to Teresa, in his last will and testament. Would you object if they became a couple and moved to Ireland?"

"Oh, my God. No. I should be very sad to see them leave the country, but I know they are in love. They have talked to Father Doyle about marriage. Danny could work on the Liffey River."

Lucia had been listening in.

"Can I be bridesmaid and travel to Ireland with them?"

Maria said, "I need you here, darling, to cheer me up. Don't forget you want to be a teacher when you grow up and study at the London University."

Jonathan guffawed. "Chance would be a fine thing."

Three Golden Balls

Jonathan made his way to the nearest shop with three golden balls hanging over the doorway. He was determined to raise a little money to buy a dress for Maria in the second-hand shop.

The marriage of Danny and Teresa in St George's Cathedral was only a week away. His dear wife must not appear moth-eaten and discoloured and old-fashioned at the wedding.

The pawnbroker might offer him a few coppers for many different things – his tools, his old leather jacket, a knife or the family shillelagh.

Jonathan still wore his father's old opal tie-pin. That would raise a few coppers and he could redeem it when the George Inn paid for his work in the stables. He would often comb and groom the horses.

Maria was amazed when he offered her the money.

"I pawned Father's tie-pin."

"Oh, thank you, darling. I always thought opals were unlucky. I was going to hide under my old bonnet and a shawl to cover the wreckage."

Maria went to the bazaar on Regent Street, foraged in one of the second-hand shops and found a lovely dark blue velvet gown that had never been worn.

"I will give you this artificial flower to wear in your hair, Madam. You cannot go barefoot to your son's wedding. You have been very honest with me about money. If you are willing to help me in the shop for a couple of hours, I will give you this pair of shoes."

"Thank you, thank you, Madam."

The deal was done and a week or two later Jonathan wore his opal tie-pin again.

The family was happy once more – again and again and again.

Felix had been given greasepaint by the manager of the South London Palace of Varieties. Thanks to him the Kellys had acquired a shaving mirror to scrape the stubble off the chin and tart up the face.

"The gin palaces have gas lighting and plate glass windows. Rum shrub is rum served with lemon and sugar. Gin is still a penny a glass. Thank the Lord, I can still afford to buy a drink without having kittens when I learn the price. You might be excited by cage-fighting – two men lashing out at one another. They may be naked. Even I don't know if it is really wrestling or fighting."

"I would not give a damn," Maria replied, " it sounds like a crazy form of suicide.

The night before the wedding, Danny washed his body with a bucket-full of almost boiling water. Jonathan heated it on a wood fire in the yard to kill any bugs from the River Thames. The boys often had just a "lick and a promise".

Danny cut a painful corn on one of his little toes and made it bleed. He used a kitchen knife for his chiropody.

"Thanks a lot. Good night, Dad."

He lay on the floor, wrapped in a length of clean hessian.

Teresa washed her Titian locks and rolled the ringlets on little bits of cotton. Flower perfume lay on the dressing-table, a present from brother Stanislaus, to make her smell sweet tomorrow. She was awake half the night, but her big sister, Angelina, slept like a log.

Father Doyle climbed into bed. Tomorrow would be the wedding of the Kellys and the O'Haras. Love and marriage in the eyes of God.

He would spend the weekend at Claremont, begging from the kings, queens and Catholic aristos for St George's Cathedral.

On the wedding day, Maria dressed and gazed at her reflection in an old glass mirror.

Was it time to search for Bella-donna eye-drops to enlarge her pupils and some rose colouring for her lips? She decided to remain bare-faced. Jonathan saw his lovely wife draped in midnight blue. Her alabaster skin glowed in the moonlight.

Maria learned how to behave correctly when she worked as a maid in the Irish mansion of an English Lord near Waterford. A teenager, in those days, but she still remembered it well.

She worried about her children's table manners, especially at the wedding breakfast. They had eaten so little for years, often with their fingers and out of old newspapers. They might talk with their mouths full, sit with their elbows on the table, use the wrong knives and forks.

"If there is any asparagus pick it up with your fingers or the tongs. Never cut it up into little pieces with your knife."

Michael O'Hara had hired two men to bring Angelina's goodies to the table, serve the wedding breakfast, clear and wash up.

The long, Georgian, mahogany diner would be set with spring flowers and candelabra that gave a golden glow.

"You must pick up a delicate porcelain cup by the handle and stick out your dinky."

Maria was trying to be firm with the boys and girls, but they were laughing their heads off.

"Shut up, you silly idiots. Your dinky is your little finger."

Danny said, "That's a relief, Mum. I thought you meant a balancing act with my willie. It might give everyone a surprise if I waved that in the air at my own wedding breakfast. What's the right word – premature?"

"You are being a silly sod, Danny. I want to tell you all something else, so listen to me for two minutes. Remember that fish knives and forks are a different shape from the others. Use your linen napkins to wipe your dirty mouths and remember it is common to call them 'serviettes'.

"Hired men will pour the booze into your glasses. I dare you to get pissed. I am sure there will be sherry, white and red wine and bubbly, followed by liqueurs. Advocaat is fashionable."

The wedding was in springtime. Father Doyle married the young couple, gave them his blessing and joined the family to celebrate.

Before the ceremony two old men on a street corner burst into raucous laughter.

"I bet they are both virgins of this parish."

Danny overheard and was longing to shut their gobs, but Stanislaus restrained him. "Ignore the drunken slobs."

Teresa wore a long gown with a silken skirt and a lace bodice. She was crowned with her late mother's small crochet shawl and a white rosebud. Pearl earrings pierced her delicate lobes, a gift from her father. Danny saved pennies from his wages as a docker to buy a dark suit for the first time in his life. He rescued a shirt and shoes from a market stall and Stanislaus gave him an emerald green velvet tie.

Thank God, Michael was able to pay for his daughter's wedding without going bankrupt. He always kept a thick wad of money in the safe of the villa and earned a fair wage as a self-employed wharfinger. Before the English became overwhelming in Eire, his family had owned a great deal of property, houses, acres of homeland, enough animals to feed a village and a small castle.

Now he hired a carriage for the close relatives to travel to and from St George's Cathedral. Michael had invited Father Doyle to join them at the wedding breakfast and he was delighted to accept. The priest made a loving speech.

"I know that one of the O'Haras, a Canty, lived in the west of Ireland and was a baird to the Kings, singing about the history of the Celts. I have read a few of your poems, Teresa, and one day I think you may write like the other Canty. You could be a wife, a mother and a poetess.

"We all grow up some time, if we are lucky enough to survive in this cruel world of illness and starvation. Praise be to the Lord, we shall never forget the Battle of the Boyne."

Later he was talking, quietly, to Michael over a cup of black coffee. "I can still enjoy weddings, even some funerals, and my begging voyages. I am a very lucky man, with friends across Europe. It is a little confusing now; there are so many different countries, with new rulers: Russia, Bavaria, Turkey and France to name a few. Schleswig-Holstein. Etcetera – etcetera." The family and friends trooped back to the house on Bandyleg Walk for the wedding breakfast.

Angelina had baked a cake and decorated it with candles and white icing. Stanislaus served buns dowsed in ale, sweet and savoury pies and petits fours.

Everyone drank wine, Irish whiskey or orange squash. No one swilled absinthe, "the green fairy".

Felix rocked on a swing in the back garden of the villa, nibbled his slice of wedding cake and hummed a tune. He had little in common with these grown-ups, although he loved them all. Later that evening he sang "Danny Boy" while Michael O'Hara accompanied him, softly, on the baby grand piano.

Paddy, the lurcher, came to the wedding dressed to kill. He wore a frilly, white ruff and a diamond-studded collar. Maria made it with glass beads and created a patchwork jacket from some old rags in the litter bin.

He sat at the head of the table with Michael, looking as proud as Punch. Lucia stroked his muzzle and Paddy licked her cheek. "He's kissing me!"

Maria said, "He might have been the best man."

A bowl of dog food was crowned with a bone created by Angelina from white icing sugar.

Stanislaus had adopted Madeleine, the stray black pussycat, and brought her to the wedding feast in a large wicker hamper. She lay under the refectory table, squinting at Paddy, the lurcher, and nibbling an oyster. A very posh animal.

The night ended with a sing-song round the grand piano. Father Doyle's voice rang out in "Ave Maria".

Three o'clock in the morning: some of the men were wobbly on their feet.

It was time to go home and leave the young lovers to their first night in bed together.

The families and dockers scattered and abandoned the wharfinger's house at last.

Maria was in floods of tears; she felt as if she were losing a child.

The only honeymoon would be a night by the River Thames. Honey by Moonlight.

Teresa undressed in the bathroom and donned her pale lemon nightgown. She gazed at her wedding ring and murmured again, "You know I shall always kiss you Good Night."

A tiny shamrock was embroidered on one pillowcase and a four-leaf clover on another. Stanislaus had painted a horseshoe for luck, over the bedroom door.

They lay in the marriage bed. Teresa was shy; she turned her back on Danny and gazed out of the window at the dark night sky and the crescent moon.

He stroked her slim silhouette. She trembled in thin air and turned towards him.

His penis brushed against her tummy. Danny mounted Teresa and they became one.

A few drops of blood from her maidenhead stained the Irish linen sheets.

An hour later Danny asked, "May I do it again?"

Two lovers meet. *Romeo and Juliet*. Ecstasy.

He kissed her gently on the mouth, licked her ears and sucked her nipples like a baby breast-feeding.

Daniel said, "I have found the love of my life."

She whispered softly, "So have I."

They slept, curved like a rainbow. Pink, yellow and blue.

Angelina knocked on the door at eight o'clock in the morning.

"Would you like a cup of tea?"

She shivered at the sight of Danny, barefoot, in his one and only nightshirt.

"I will leave you in peace."

Angie scuttled back to the kitchen.

Nine months later the twins, Ricky and Vicky, were born in the villa on Bandyleg Walk.

The midwife said, "She is a very young mother and seems to be healthy. I am sure there is no need for a hospital visit.

Teresa and Daniel sat in the living-room; they cuddled one baby each. The infants were wrapped in shawls knitted by Maria and Angelina. Grandfather Michael had bought the lambs' wool and knitting needles.

"They are lovely babes. Their other grandmother would have been so proud of them."

Richard and Victoria – another Queen of England.

They laughed and rejoiced when Father Doyle baptised the little ones.

The boy had dark curly hair and brown eyes. The little girl was like her mummy, with Titian red hair and deep blue peepers.

"You might have quads next time, even five at a time. What do they call that?"

"I'm not bothered, but I think it's quintuplets. I can cope with two at a time although breast-feeding can be difficult. We are lucky to live so near the pumps. There is plenty of clean water to wash me and the twins."

Angelina was always willing to help in any way but her own life was never physical.

She was happy to be the family's cook, cleaner and washerwoman.

When the twins were a year old they sailed to Ireland with their parents to live in Grandfather's log cabin in Dublin.

They caught a train from Southwark to the West Country, changing en route.

Michael said, "Promise me you will often come back to England and bring the brood. I must try not to be selfish, but it is a lonely life without your mother." He sighed. "Felix and Stanislaus are crazy about their work and you know Angelina will be a nun. I am lucky in so many ways. I love my life as a wharfinger on the river; I shall not leave England for a while. Southwark is fascinating; there are so many nationalities, Italian, French, Bavarians, Phillipinos and many mixed race immigrants. They tell me some of them were prisoners of war."

After a long, tiring train journey across England the family embarked on board ship and set sail. Privacy came at a price, but they had been able to lock the carriage door on the train and kiss one another good night.

The young couple could see the hills of Erin rising in the light grey mist of a spring morning. It would soon be time to visit Bray and Glendalough and recall the history they learned at school and at their mothers' knees.

Another world of fairy stories.

Daniel and Teresa gazed at the lovely shrines to Our Lady by the wayside.

Fresh flowers from the grass verge and the gardens of worshippers, some resting at the foot of a wooden cross.

It was early spring; daffodils, snowdrops and bluebells created many lovely posies.

Red and yellow roses, camellias and a water lily floating in a Waterford glass bowl.

Maria had knitted an emerald green woollen coat for Paddy the lurcher to wear on his journey to Ireland.

"We don't want him to catch cold. He was the one who introduced Danny and Teresa."

The lurcher had long brindle hair with a few dark spots. He was a cross-breed with a greyhound and a hunting dog. One of his ancestors might have been a poacher, stealing fish and game from the wealthy.

He crossed the Irish Sea without being sick in his basket.

Teresa asked Danny, "Have you heard of Cruft's Dog

Show? One day I would love to go there. It is organised by Charles Cruft – and known as Cruft's Dog Show International Society. They run it in Islington every February; I think the first one was in 1884."

"You do rattle on, darling. I think I'm going to be sea-sick at any minute."

The family reached the harbour without any problems. The twins slept most of the way and Teresa read from a book by Charles Dickens.

Thank the Lord for George Stephenson and his railways. Now one could catch a train across England and board a liner to Dublin.

It had been a rough, old day. Their bellies lurched but they were happy to eat as soon as they reached dry land.

They travelled past a gypsy encampment to reach Dublin.

A coach carried the family over the bridge to the cottage beside the River Liffey.

"What shall we call it? Twinny Cottage?"

"That is a daft idea. Dante Cottage would be far better. A puzzle for ordinary blokes, yet it joins our names together – Danny and Teresa. Poor Teresa! You will be head cook and bottle-washer, and nursemaid to the twins."

"That's not all. I would love to write in my spare time."

Danny bent down and kissed her gently on the cheek. She was cuddling Ricky.

"Sorry, darling, but I don't think you will have a great deal of time to spare." He laughed. "You know I would love to fight for a free Ireland but I dare not risk spending a few years in Kilmainham Gaol. We shall see, darling, we shall see."

He had found an important letter of Granddad's but it was not a good time to take orders now.

Fianna

Grandfather O'Hara lay back in his wing chair gazing across Dublin Harbour. The sun was dying and so was he. Doctors at the hospital had promised him a few more days on this earth.

Grandfather grasped a quill pen with his gnarled fingers and wrote his last letter to Teresa and Daniel.

The log cabin and its contents would be inherited by the children he had never met.

He longed for a free Ireland, without the dominance of English soldiers and wardens. Danny might take up arms and fight the invaders.

"Remember the Vikings, the Battle of the Boyne and Oliver Cromwell in Youghal. Years ago there were many kings of Ireland. Danny boy, I am sure you will battle for freedom.

"Listen to O'Connell, the Liberator. One day I know there will be an uprising against the Orange Men. We all want to believe we are descendants of King Brian Bohru, who was crowned on the Hill of Tara.

"Pray God, my youngsters and their children will have the courage to fight.

"Always remember your Grandfather, Liam O'Hara, was a Fenian. Finn was a mythical warrior.

"My life in this world is almost over, otherwise I could

have taught you to make a petrol bomb.
God bless you all.
Liam O'Hara"

★★★

The walls of Dante Cottage were painted white and pale grey; the curtains green damask. There were wooden candle sconces on all the walls. The kitchen equipment was different from anything at home in Southwark.

One evening she said, "I have heard of Dante Gabriel from my brother but I know there was another who was far more famous. He was an Italian poet, many, many years ago. Dante Alighieri. I think he was born in the thirteenth century and dreamed of a great Empire.

It would be an honour to call our residence Dante's Cottage."

They both laughed at the grandeur of the poet's history. Their new home lay in a working-class area near the harbour. Two bedrooms, a living-room, and furniture fit for the swells. A tall, oak dresser crowned with "pot and porc", chairs and a settee with down and feathers flying out of needlework cushions.

A double bed with plush curtains and a commode full of the Liffey water. A bucket was too heavy for Teresa to lift but Danny coped with the pump.

The little ones peered down a well in the street and the mother was terrified they might lose their balance, fall in and drown. A bacon box in front of the log fire could act as a crib for the twins.

Danny might work as a docker or a coachman. When Grandfather Liam knew he had only a few months to live and was on the skids he had left a list of likely bosses in the larder.

Sometimes Father Kelly had talked about Shanigan's Old Shabeen. It sounded like a grand mansion but it was only a whiskey shop.

One evening Ricky was longing for a hug. He lay on the settee cuddled up in his mother's arms; as snug as a bug in a rug. Vicky was playing ball on the floor.

Danny said, "Be careful, little one, you might bounce it too high and break one of Mummy's ornaments." Granddad's collection of Wedgewood jugs and vases decorated the room.

"It's nearly tea-time, Ricky. I expect your dad's starving. We've got pork and pease pudding tonight. You know it's our weekend treat."

Teresa loved her new life in this cabin by the River Liffey. The following day the sun was blazing on the water. The kids sucked their lollipops while Danny and Teresa waltzed across the sand in one another's arms.

Paddy the lurcher met a stray bitch on the streets of Dublin and she gave birth to a fine litter of pups in the garden shed. Teresa made up a bed with old blankets and a pillow. (The little ones might have been suffocated but they all survived the loving care.) Three mongrel pups joined the Kelly-O'Haras.

One day two pigeons were making love on the roof of the cabin, kissing one another, beak to beak. Suddenly a giant bird fluttered out of the sky on to the young ones, attacking them, and they flew away, but came back an hour or two later and had sex. Soon a nest was built under the eaves and baby birds were fed.

Teresa was talking to the twins at bedtime.

"My daddy always said, 'There are fairies at the bottom of our garden.' One night I crept down the path to look for them. I could see a crescent moon in the sky. Candles were alight under the bushes and two tiny figurines were lying in the long grass, fast asleep.

"Silver stars shone in their long, red curly hair. Suddenly one leapt to her feet saying, 'Dance with me, Ricky.' She was wearing a powder blue tutu and twirled on little black ballet shoes. The fairy boy was dressed in green velvet pants. He said, 'Waltz with me, Vicky,' and clasped her tiny waist. They danced away towards the river then swam off into the night. Now you know why I called you Ricky and Vicky, my fairy children."

Danny broke into her story, "May I be King of the Fairies, my Teresa?"

"You always have been, my darling."

He laughed.

"We are a couple of daft buggers, aren't we?"

He bent down to kiss his wife and children good night.

It was bedtime for all the boys and girls.

Teresa was reading an old poem aloud to Danny.

> *"When e'er such wanderers I meet*
> *As from their nightsports they trudge home*
> *With counterfeiting voice I greet,*
> *And call them on, with me to roame*
> *Through woods, through lakes,*
> *Through bogs, through brakes;*
> *Or else, unseen, with them I go,*
> *All in the nicke,*
> *To play some trick*
> *And frolicke it, with ho, ho, ho!"*

Teresa tucked the twins, Ricky and Vicky, up in their little beds saying: "Tonight your bedtime story will be another Irish fairy tale. It is quite different from 'Cinderella' with the lost slipper and the ugly sisters.

This is the story of the Priest's Supper.
The fairies were dancing in the open air, by moonlight.
'Come, come with your drumming
Here's an end to our mumming.
By my smell
I can tell
A priest this way is coming'.

Teresa gazed up into the Heavens and sighed. "I still believe all the stories I was told as a little one. Father Horrigan rose his pony to a log cabin and entered saying: 'My blessing on all here.

It was the home of Dermot Leary and he realised the priest intended to stay the night. The family meal would have been potatoes and a red apple, but Dermot had set a net in the river to catch fish. This would be far more palatable for the Father. He ran to the riverside, longing to offer the wandering priest good food. A fine salmon lay at the bottom of the net, but it escaped from his groping hands and swam away. One of the many fairies dancing by the waterside called out to Dermot, 'Go and ask Father Horrigan to tell us whether our souls will be saved at the last day, like the souls of good Christians, only; if you wish us well, bring back word what he says without delay. Then we will provide a magical supper, a meal from fairyland.'

When the priest got the message, second-hand, from the fairies, he suggested they should come to him and ask their questions about this world and the next.

"Everyone enjoyed their simple meal, while dozens of fairies played and danced on the waterfront and in the sky above the cabin."

Tomorrow another fish might lie in the net and Daniel would sell it on the market and feed the family.

"Bell, book and candle shall not drive me back
When gold and silver becks me to come one."

The twins had fallen asleep long ago; the whole story was far too grown-up for toddlers who were only 3 years old.

It was a bad choice, but Danny sat holding his wife's hands in his, fascinated by her Irish fairy tale.

"I know you want to write romantic love stories; I only hope I am one of your heroes." He laughed. "When you are free from this domestic life, I can imagine you studying at the University of Dublin."

He raised his glass of ale in the air.

"Thank God I'm not on the wagon; I would have fallen off years ago."

She kissed his cheek. "You are not a binge-drinker, darling. That has never appealed to you."

She sipped a glass of sherry standing on a nearby table.

"You know I would love to go to one of the two Dublin universities in the years to come. They tell me that Trinity favours Protestant students although I think the law was altered in 1870."

It was nearly bedtime and Danny was feeling garrulous after imbibing a couple of pints of ale.

"You and Stanislaus are far more artistic than any of our family. I know Angelina is pious. That is not meant to be a put-down; I respect any girl who has the courage to become a nun. She divorces herself from a normal life, loving a man and their children. You know my family has always been forced to be more practical than yours. They all love skating on the Thames in wintertime. The Ma can make a meal out of old scraps of food – like pig swill. I suppose it has always been their sheer determination to survive. I think I inherited that, I will make a good living for my children."

"Your golden twins, Ricky and Vicky. Richard and Victoria."

"Thank God, we don't need to analyse every action, it would be exhausting."

Teresa yawned. It had been a tiring day and she was ready for her bed. She covered her mouth with tapering fingers. Danny must not realise she was exhausted. He prattled on.

"You know my little sister called herself Rosa in Wonderland after that book she read with Stanni. Living here we can spend days on the cliffs at Bray overlooking the water. They say the view is fantastic. There is transport to Glendalough where a hermit slept on a ledge above the lake."

Teresa said, "I shall never forget the tall fuchsia hedges beside the country land in Erin and the West of England. The purple and golden flowers are so lovely. Our Lady's Eardrops."

Danny took a slurp of Irish Whiskey he had found in Liam O'Hara's cellar. It may have been the old boy's influence, from another world.

"One day the whole of Ireland will be free. God knows we don't want to live under foreign rule, be it Spanish or English. We are Celtic, with our own moral code and way of life."

Daniel raised his glass to his wife.

"Schlainte!"

Daniel beamed. "I suppose I could be a gardener or a ranger at Phoenix Park. I would love to work with wild animals. The kids could come in free to ride on the camels and feed the giraffes and ostriches. There are nearly 200 acres round the vice-regal residence and several other grand buildings."

The twins stirred. Ricky was bobbing up and down. "Phoenix, Mummy. What's a phoenix?"

"It's a fairy bird, with lovely feathers. Sometimes it lives for 500 years or more."

Fianna

"Coo!"

"You would have to behave yourself in the park, kids. No shenanigans."

"They are too young to know the meaning of the word." His wife laughed. "Your two golden angels."

Teresa told the twins bedtime stories about the Dolphins of Dingle Bay, the King of the Leprechauns on the Hill of Kerry, angels floating in the air and the horses galloping in the sky.

Years later Ricky became a jockey, still dreaming of life in another world. He rode in the Curragh and at Newmarket, but he was always a rank outsider.

Vicky worked as a needlewoman for a shop off Grafton Street.

Teresa remembered her ambition in life and began to write romantic novels and children's stories. One night she and Danny met a publisher, a friend of Grandfather's, in the Shelbourne Hotel and, after reading several chapters, he was fascinated by her work.

★★★

The Crimean War broke out in 1854; we were allies of the Turks against the Russians. There was an appeal for priests and nuns to work in the battlefield.

Father Doyle spoke about this at a Requiem Mass in St George's. Doyle said, "The church was very well attended, and many prayers were offered for the souls of the brave men who have fallen under the late strokes of war and disease. We want more priests for the army, there is not any doubt. Well and good, and for the navy we have none. It is a dreadful state of things, dreadful, frightful. What is wanted now are more priests for the forces; they are wanted now – well, give me them now, and I will doff my cap and bow down to an angle of forty-five, and call you my very fair and gentle masters."

The Sisters of Mercy responded to the call for nurses, under the leadership of Florence Nightingale, and Doyle wrote: "Quick march – forward. Last Sunday night the second division of our good nuns received orders to set out for the East, and on Monday morning, at six o'clock, they were here and on their knees before the altar, the source of strength and happiness; and at seven off by the express to Paris. God be with them. The force is not strong in numbers – only five. Last week five others had gone forth from Bermondsey, and with the same despatch and hearty willingness.

"The last five came from the Convent of Norwood, and another party are ready to follow them. Thus ten nuns are now on their way to the East, and may every blessing go with them."

The Rev. James Doyle, the Provost's brother, had charge of the missions at Chatham and Kingston-on-Thames. He left his church and travelled to the war.

Father Doyle paid a tribute to Father Wheble who had been sent to St. George's to commence his work as a priest. Father Wheble fell and died at Balaclava.

★★★

Father Doyle was talking to his hostess, Lady Petre, at Ingatestone Hall, about twenty-five miles north of London. They were sitting in the drawing-room of the mansion in front of a blazing, golden log fire.

"You know the People's Princess, Caroline, married Leopold of Saxe-Coburg before I came to Southwark from St Edmund's College, Ware. She had resisted a great deal of pressure from her father, Prince George, to marry the Prince of Orange.

"Her wedding gift from Parliament was Claremont House, valued at £56,000. The poor young lady died in childbirth and their baby was still-born. Her husband was broken-hearted.

"These days I am often invited to Claremont and receive many gifts from the Catholic gentry. I love to wander along the Camellia Terrace in the grounds. The dinner parties with the aristos are a godsend, the Dukes of Arundel and Newcastle are very kind-hearted, they arrange for me to travel by carriage or post chaise."

Lady Petre laughed. "I suppose you share a grand meal and suffer from indigestion for days."

"I must admit it makes a fabulous change after so much bread and cheese, but I don't feel guilty. Claremont became the residence of the Bourbon in exile, King Louis Philippe. He was always so generous, but he died in 1850. His wife, Marie Amèlie, still lives in the house."

Father soothed his throat with a drop of liquid.

"You know I am a beggar at the courts of Europe and the homes of the wealthy. The Continent is in a state of chaos, being ruled by the Tsar of Russia, Italy and Saxe-Coburg. I have never travelled on the gentleman's Grand Tour, but you know I sail and ride many carriages in many countries. I journeyed to Rome with my begging bowl.

"My mission in life is to collect money for the Cathedral of St George, the poor living on the streets of London and the praise of God. I remember bowing to His Majesty King Ludwig of Bavaria and saying, 'You do me a great honour, Your Majesty. I am a beggar, a slave to the poor people of England and Ireland.'"

Another journey. Father Doyle was staying with his friends the Petres at Ingatestone Hall, when he said, "I am sure you have met Daniel O'Connell. He is an M.P. in England, but in Ireland he is known as The Liberator. He fights for Irish freedom against the union with this country.

Several years ago he held a meeting on the hill of Tara where Brian Bohru was crowned King of Ireland, hundreds of years ago (he defeated the Vikings and married one of their princesses).

Daniel planned another meeting and thousands were coming to Clontarf, but the English government intervened and forbade it. They threatened Daniel with punishment for being anti-English. The demonstration was cancelled but the imprisonment was carried out. The English sent him to gaol for one year. The governor of Bridewell Prison entertained Daniel in his own private home and he lived in comfort with his family to keep him company. Now he comes to support us at St George's, a few months after his release. We are all proud to be Irish, although my young brother and I were born in England, of Irish parentage.

In 1823 Daniel O'Connell had set up a Catholic Association in Ireland with Richard Lalor Shiel to obtain Catholic Emancipation. It met with fantastic support in Leinster and Munster. Catholic rent of a penny a month would fund the action.

Daniel became an M.P. in 1829 when he was fifty-five and by 1841 he was Mayor of Dublin.

In May 1846 he was in the chair at the annual dinner on behalf of the Southwark Charity Schools. Now only £3,000 is required to complete the work on the church. ERIN GO BRACH!

"Where does the money come from? From the warm and faithful hearts of Erin's children."

In his after-dinner speech O'Connell said, "A well-earned meed of praise to the lively, energetic, zealous Dr Doyle, whose exertions on behalf of the noble Cathedral of St George are so well known.

"It would seem a kind of retribution if this noble Catholic structure should rise in the very spot where Lord George Gordon assembled his lunatic mob in the last century and urged them on to their work of devastation and plunder of the Catholics."

In July 1852, Father Doyle received an honour for which, as one of the leading and best-known priests of London and of the new diocese of Southwark, he was eminently fitted.

On the 2nd July the first Chapter of Southwark was created.

In August, the Superioress of the Convent at Norwood, in which Dr Doyle took such a great interest, was charged with the alleged ill-treatment of a child in her care, and Dr Doyle wrote: "St George's and the Convent of Our Lady at Norwood. Both establishments are in Southwark, and both bid fair for descending the stream of time as places worth remembering, so an account of the recent trial at Guildford…"

Father Thomas sat at nearly the whole of the trial.

The morning of August 5th was indeed an anxious one; what a painful position for those poor ladies. What a contrast to their quietude and seclusion at Norwood.

"The silent chapel, retired house and holy cloister for a public court of justice, crowded with all sorts of people, and with a judge and jury prepared to condemn them, for so a recent trial lead them to think. Add to this their extreme anguish of heart at the amazing ingratitude of their accuser, and yet her ingratitude was the least of their troubles for her. The affair of the cross-examination they had yet to learn."

He then described in detail the ordeal of the Superioress, who was in the witness box for five or six hours under cross-examination, which attempted to bring ridicule upon her mode of life, but the case ended in the complete vindication of the Convent.

Later the Doctor wrote: "What are we Catholics to do under the bitter feelings of this land, where men with no religion tolerate us, but where men and women of a religious cast and observance do tolerate us because they are obliged, but would sink the whole family of us in the Red Sea, if they could; who loathe and hate us as enemies of the Gospel, and regard us as sons of Belial. We are in the midst of people who do not understand us."

★★★

Michael and Angelina were talking in the garden.

"Your mummy and I were so happy together. It was the shock of my life when she died."

"I know that's true, Daddy, but I want to help the sick and the poor to lead a better life and serve God. Even the waifs and strays from St Patrick's in Soho give pennies to the Cathedral of St George and the poor Irish."

"You know we have been very lucky, darling. I might have been slave labour if we had stayed in Ireland."

"Father Doyle tells me his brother was a priest at Chatham and Kingston-on-Thames. There is a French Convent near the sea in Brighton. Southwark is in the same diocese."

"You know we will help you in any way we can. Thank God we are not living on the bread line, like the poor devils in the slums."

"I can understand how you feel, Daddy. There are Sisters of Mercy living under a rule. The Daughters of Charity were established by St Vincent de Paul in 1633. They nurse the sick, teach and help the poor. I have learned so much from Father Doyle. He is a wonderful man, born in England and educated at St Edmund's College, Ware. His parents are Irish. Have you heard him sing? He has a lovely voice."

★★★

Jonathan had a great week; he earned six pennies grooming the horses of a very famous, wealthy gentleman.

"We can have our night on the tiles. Let's take the kids to see Felix work his act in St James's Park. I know it only lasts a few minutes but it will be a great treat for them."

Lucia rode on Daddy's shoulders.

Jonathan watched the boy.

"He might be lucky enough to pull it off, one day."

A neighbour in the stalls said, "You can always tell the wheat from the chaff."

A middle-aged Yank joined in the conversation saying, "That kid's got talent. They would love him in the States, I will see what I can organise. I might be able to book him a short tour next year. He looks bloody good, too. I like the patent leather hair and a few curls on his chest. They peep out from his shirt."

Jonathan said, "The kid's my son. Don't get ideas, he's not going on the game."

The Yank said, "Don't worry, old boy, that's not my line of country."

One of the Southwark street urchins was skulking under the trees. He knew Felix when they were school boys, but he had given up education ages ago.

Now he latched on to the Kellys hoping for a free glass of lemonade and a currant bun.

"Hullo, Felix. Remember me? We were at St Patrick's School together."

No reaction from the family.

The show was over.

★★★

The old boy who lived behind the Kellys kicked the bucket. He had survived for weeks on a barrel of ale and a few chunks of stale bread. His allowance of three shillings a week had been cut to one.

Was the cause of his death starvation? Had he caught the clap in his younger days? (This was always called Le Clapoir by Le Vicomte.)

No one gave a damn about yet another poverty-stricken Irish man.

If Father Doyle had encountered him and known of his condition the poor old boy would have been sent to the workhouse, or given a few pence to help him survive.

Instead his body was carted off to the nearest burial ground.

It was the dead of night when someone climbed through a broken gap in one wall of the hovel.

He coughed and spat.

The place stank of sewage, piss and puss; a privy pail had not been emptied for weeks on end.

The young boy gazed around; he had found a home at last.

Freddie Reilly made up his mind to share it with the bugs and lice, shiny black cockroaches and spiders.

He would kill them off, bit by bit.

Were these called harvest spiders?

Dear God, he was as ignorant as a pig.

One of his bare feet trod on an insect and killed it. He knew Irish superstition said this was unlucky.

To Hell with all that.

A pair of dark red slippers lay on the floor. He tried

them on, but they were far too big, he slipped on the rotten floorboards.

There was a small hole on the inside wall. Ever inquisitive, Freddie gawped through it, but got the shock of his life.

Another pair of eyes met his own.

It was bedtime for the Kellys, but Felix was the last to go to sleep.

He had been practising a few dance steps, using an old wooden towel rail as a barre.

The hole in the rotten wooden wall that divided some of the back-to-back hovels was a gross disappointment.

Freddie wanted a free view of some sexual activity; the sight of Jonathan's penis or someone masturbating?

When Felix caught him peering through the gap he said, "Fuck off, Freddie."

Several years ago they had been in the same class at school. Tomorrow he would block the hole with sodden old newspapers and cardboard.

The two boys were both starving hungry.

"Have you ever tried to grow potatoes, Felix? I could sell you one for a penny; I nicked it from a stall on the market. The old girl couldn't run fast enough to catch me."

"I saw the mother plant one in a cardboard box, sideways, with a little mound of earth on top. It caught the blight and went rotten; even the leaves curled up and died."

"I'm half Italian. My Father came from Naples but he died years ago and Ma did a bunk."

Freddie was determined not to grow up as one of the great unwashed. He would do anything to escape from this dreary way of life: steal, rape, marry for money, become a pimp or a hit man.

Felix thought he might end up in Marshalsea Prison with a gang of criminals.

"See you tomorrow, boy." Freddie lay on the bare boards and fell asleep.

One night he made a pass at his Irish friend.

Felix said, "Get stuffed, boy. No, I don't mean in that way."

"Goodbye, now."

Freddie told Felix "You can buy 'the green fairy' for coppers on almost every street corner in London. Its real name is absinthe. I thought it was a drug you either sniffed or smoked, but it's a green liqueur. We might try it one of these days. Someone told me it can affect the mind and the body; that sounds quite exciting."

"Thanks, but no thanks."

"Some people call it wormwood, but it's the same thing."

"I have been offered laudanum; I know that's opium, in dirty brown liquid. Barrow boys sold swigs when we went to Covent Garden, but Dad refused. He's not an old druggie. I can't cope with all that rubbish; I don't want to die in my teens. I can't think where you get some of these crazy ideas, wanting to experiment with any old thing. Wormwood makes me think of slugs and worms crawling around in my tummy."

"Don't forget I grew up in the workhouse, ducky, I was in the workhouse for years, but I escaped. I nearly ended up in Dr Barnardo's, but I bolted and they couldn't find me. Otherwise I might be on my way to Canada with thousands of others. I suppose anything might be better than this god-awful hole."

★★★

The weeks flew past in the Kelly hovel.

Lucia was squeaking and squawling like the chickens in the pub yard and the roosters.

Jonathan roared at the infant in the middle of the night.

"Shut up, you little monkey. I can't get a wink of sleep."

Felix was snoring.

A few minutes deathly silence, then the little one, Lucia, was off again. A noise to lift the rafters.

One afternoon Freddie said, casually, "I thought I might murder one or two old girls and steal their jewellery and any money they had left lying around."

He laughed. "I quite fancy a pearl stomacher or a diamond tiara."

"Don't be an idiot, Freddie."

"I'm deadly serious. I would hide in the kitchen and poison them. I think arsenic is the favourite; it's dead cheap and very easy to come by. All you have to do is buy fly papers from the chemist for a few pence and soak them in water. You will have all the poison you need. I think the victims die in agony, but I wouldn't give a damn.

"Some people do it to claim life insurance. I couldn't do that in a million years, all I want is their possessions. I would steal those."

"Don't be such a wicked sod, Freddie. You would end your life in Newgate Gaol, hanging by the neck behind closed doors."

"Blimey O'Reilly! I don't give a damn. I would rather be hung, drawn and quartered than end my life in the poor house. I thought about working on a liner and sailing to Italy, but I changed my mind. I long for a new life in America."

"You have got brawn and brains, Freddie. Why not choose the good life for a change?"

"That's strange, Felix. Father Doyle said exactly the same thing when he caught me prowling round the cathedral. I was never brought up as a Roman Catholic; I was dragged up in the gutter."

"I suppose I am dead lucky; my one and only ambition is to spend all my life working in the theatre," said Felix.

A few days later the two boys were perched on a bench by the riverside, munching odds and sods Felix had found in Maria's larder cupboard.

Freddie swept a few stale grey crumbs from his tatty black trousers saying, "I was starving!"

They both shivered, the weather was damp and cold.

"Yesterday I made a pass at a girl called Annie. It wasn't passion, I thought it might warm me up, but the silly bitch wouldn't play ball. I did quite fancy her round boobs and bum, so I shoved her to the ground in the bushes near the river. It would have hidden us from any passers-by.

"She screamed 'Piss off. My mum had the pox; you might catch it from me.' I pulled away and let her stand on her own two feet. I wonder if she's caught syphilis or gonorrhoea?"

"You pretend to be an expert on sex, Freddie. Don't you know anything about V.D.? Anyway, the girl warned you off. I'm sure you don't want to catch the clap."

Felix would not tell him the truth, it might be dangerous for the little girl; she could become pregnant in days. Annie knew she could trust Felix with her secrets. The previous week she had visited the hospital and they had given her the 'all clear'.

Freddie said, "V.D. sounds like a game."

"I suppose it does. A doctor told me signs appear about three weeks after infection. So, watch out before you go astray again."

"Balls to you, young man. You might end up as queer as a coot, and hang on the roof of Horsemonger's Gaol."
Freddie and Felix were chatting on the street... again.

"I help clean out the carriages at the George Inn and nick anything I can lay my hands on. I'm not going to end up in the workhouse like my poor old granddad. I'd rather be a hit man and kill for money. One day I stole a pair of cuff-links and a load of clobber. A swell had it off with a street girl and ended up half-naked. He must have been as drunk as a fart.

"You can sell almost anything on the Covent Garden Square; I would like a stall on the market, or a shop in a posh bazaar. We might work together, Felix?"

Felix warbled a little tune. "I think I will stay with the music."

Freddie broke in.

"I had another idea. I could stow away on a ship to America, join a gang out there and make a fortune. We might meet one day; me stinking rich and you trying to entertain on Broadway."

"I should talk to Father Doyle before you do a bunk to the States."

The mafia or the music hall?

In the meantime the stage manager at the South London Palace of Varieties had arranged music lessons for Felix. Now he knew the difference between sharps and flats and could even play a few notes on the harmonica.

★★★

It was a cold winter's night with a heavy rainfall.

Four boys hid under the willow trees round the burial ground. One careful little bugger wore a pair of his mother's moth-eaten woolly gloves, another his dad's torn leather mitts.

It was a filthy job, handling bones and the rotten flesh of the disintegrating cadavers. Some had lain in the burial ground a long while; the blood and guts were rotten.

The kids are digging up skeletons in the pouring rain, but they didn't care? The surgeons at the hospitals needed them to dissect and would pay good money for the privilege.

The four boys fetched their trolley from among the bushes, loaded their filthy treasures sky-high and covered everything with an old blanket. If a Metropolitan policeman should catch sight of them they would dump the lot and run like Hell. There was no evidence; they had nicked the barrow. Push and shove. It was overloaded and seemed to weigh a ton.

They reached the hospital at last, out of breath and knackered, although they had taken turns on the way along.

One of the surgeons gave money to a night nurse and she paid the kids. One boy was in charge of the deal; there were pennies for every corpse on the barrow.

Bacteria rejoiced in the youngsters' sodden clothes. They all needed to jump into battered tin baths. It would be a kind of confession to their families, who thought they were all fast asleep.

It was eleven o'clock at night – they could be drunk by midnight, party in one of the parks, or scoff chips and oysters.

They dumped the barrow in the back yard of a pub and trotted off to celebrate, and breed more material for the scalpels of the surgeons.

Embalming was a strange word, used by the upper classes. *Thank God*, thought the boys, the idea of cremation was abhorrent to all Catholics.

They might have lost all this wonderful money. "Throw your gloves in the river, boy."

★★★

Felix was sitting at the riverside reading a penny-dreadful. He felt a hand on his shoulder and ducked away, quickly.

A tall, brawny man with a coffee-coloured face hovered over him.

"I think you are Felix Kelly?"

Felix nodded. He was ready for a punch-up.

"You had a friend who was called Federico? We worked together in America, trying to raise a little money. We wanted to enjoy life for the first time, ever."

His accent was a strong as a mule.

"I had escaped from slave labour. Federico wanted me to call him Freddie – that is a strange name."

Felix was becoming aware of some evil action in this story.

"He asked me to join him in the States. Where is Freddie now? Has he come back to England? He might wash our kitchen floor for a copper or two and give Mum a break."

"Too late, my friend. Too late! He travelled to New York, Las Vegas and Los Angeles, the City of Angels. Freddie was becoming powerful in Gangland. Many were jealous of him, and someone paid a hit man to shoot him down. His dead body fell into the water. He was always aware of the danger."

"We were good friends. I am so sorry."

"He told me many stories of the life in Southwark and gave me one last task."

By now they were sitting together in the long grass.

"My name is Christian – don't laugh at me."

He drew a small black leather purse from the inner pocket of his dark jacket.

"Federico told me he always loved you, but you would never play ball. This was his last present.."

Felix opened his gift and found a rosary, a silver cross and a miniature head-and-shoulders portrait of Freddie in a black papier-mâché frame. A lovely card was painted with a white lily.

"Remember me? God Bless you, Felix. *Arrivederci!*"

There were tears in the black man's eyes.

"He was so kind to me. I shall never forget him, as long as I live."

He leaped to his feet and disappeared into the undergrowth. Felix would never see the messenger again.

He stayed by the Silent Waterway for a long while, grieving over the death of his lost friend.

He hid the precious gift in the back pocket of his pants and strolled home for tea with his family.

One night the spirit of Federico might hover in the air. Father Doyle wrote: "Don't let us look dry toast and salt fish in the mouth.

The sun is out, and the crocus and snowdrop greet us, and the sky looks blue.

Come, let us rejoice, even though milk and butter and mutton chops do not.

Puritanical long faces and lantern jaws, skimmed-milk countenances you may be sure, no doubt, are most often called gentlemen and gentle dames."

★★★

The Oxford Music Hall cost £35,000 to build but the restaurant could hold 18,000 people.

It has been known as The Bear and Castle and was erected on the corner of Oxford Street and the Tottenham Court Road.

Felix read any penny papers or magazines about the theatre, the love of his life. Of course he could never afford to buy them but sometimes old copies were dumped in the gutter.

He was crazy about one song by Leybourne. This artist could earn the equivalent of £120 a week at the opera comique. A vast fortune.

"Champagne Charlie is my name,
Champagne drinking is my game.

I don't care what becomes of me.

"Gossip said he favoured Moet et Chandon."

★★★

Renting a room in Southwark might cost two shillings a month, but food could add another seven shillings. There was a bear garden to provide entertainment.

The bear handlers often pulled out the animals' teeth and claws to protect themselves.

In 1863 Father Doyle was still scavenging for money.

He wrote: "The Church has no tower! It is like a fine body without a head.

What would you be without one? Fine limbs, but no head."

The Crimean War concluded with the Treaty of Paris in 1856. Sevastopol was named "the eye-tooth of the bear."

The Russians were forced to the conference table, and there were fireworks in London's Green Park to celebrate the victory.

Political life on the continent was chaotic in the nineteenth century.

After the Battle of Waterloo we were fighting with the Turks against the Russians. Thousands of English men died in the Charge of the Light Brigade and the Battle of Balaclava.

George, the Prince Regent, had tried to pressurise his daughter to marry the Prince of Orange, but the young lady, known as the People's Princess, fell in love with Leopold and married him instead.

He was broken-hearted when she died in childbirth, at twenty-one years of age, and he became the King of the Belgians.

The Bourbon, King Louis Philippe of France, was an exile. He lived in Twickenham for years and became a country gentleman. Louis loved his garden and animals, the Citizen King even collected horse dung from the streets to nourish his roses.

Writers, singers and diplomats joined his Royal Court and enjoyed amateur theatricals, whist drives and concerts.

Napoleon lost power and Louis returned to France, claimed some of his wealth and went back to Twickenham.

He had married Marie Amèlie, daughter of the King of Sicily, and moved to Orleans House which he rented for £250 a year.

Louis died at Claremont in 1850.

★★★

Rain was pelting down through the roof of the Kellys' hovel and Lucia caught a belting cold. She was as wet as a river fish, shivering like a leaf of paper in a high wind.

"It might become pneumonia. Do you think I should take her to hospital, Jonathan?"

"No way, darlin'. They might send you both to the poor house.

Try to give her lots of hot drinks."

The little one spat and vomited, but she was able to swallow a few drops of warm tea and soon fell asleep.

"Please God she's not in a coma."

Maria stripped Lucia and wrapped her in the old family horse blanket.

"I suppose the rest of the family might catch the bug?"

"We are all as strong as horses."

Jonathan was right and Felix was the only one to become a victim.

That night he strode on stage – all five feet five inches high – opened his mouth and a crackling sound emerged. It was rather like an old duck quacking; the youngster had lost his voice.

He was quick enough to treat it as comedy, croaked like a frog and went into his dance act.

The audience loved it, they had no idea it was a cover-up.

Laryngitis or tonsillitis? His throat was swollen like a tunnel.

Felix went home with his father, gargled with salt and water and felt as sick as a pig.

A dumb "song and dance man" would never be top of the bill, even in the London Parks, and Felix was a very ambitious young man.

Jonathan borrowed a ladder from the pub; climbed on to the roof of their wooden cabin and nailed some bits of old board across the hole.

Liquid still seeped through the cracks but it was no longer a waterfall.

A few days later life reverted to the norm for all the family. They could all talk for Ireland.

Thank God, spring was on the way.

Flossie-Bang-Bang And Pussy-Wussy

Rosa had only one toy; a bear she named Flossie-Bang-Bang.

"Why on earth have you given her such a funny name?"

"Because her ears are brown and smooth and flossy. Bang-Bang because she farts in the night. We cuddle together and she wakes me up every morning."

Maria laughed. "I think it might have been your Daddy, my Jonathan, not Flossie-Bang-Bang."

That evening Rosa was late home from school.

"I heard another superstition on the street today: 'See a pin and pick it up, all the day you'll have good luck. See a pin and let it lie, ill luck you'll have the live-long day.' Tip your old needlework basket on the floor, Mummy, and I'll pick 'em all up."

"Don't be a silly moo, darling."

Lucia called out from her blanket on the floor. "I can't get to sleep with you playing games. Do shut up. You'll wake up our Daddy, he's snoring."

Rosa picked up one of the little black and white kittens, a gift from her best friend, Uncle Stanislaus. She purred at him and listened for a reply, then stroked his ears and fluffy back.

"My little pussy-wussy. You were my present, the one with the white face, paws and whiskers. I don't think you will ever grin like the Cheshire Cat. Stay on my lap and we will sleep together on the straw in the corner. I'm dog-tired. Night, night, Mummy."

★★★

Springtime. White blossom swept over the brick walls of Lambeth Palace Garden. A cluster of bluebells edged the road and the Thames – The Silent Highway.

The Archbishop would invite many Protestant worshippers to a garden party to celebrate Saint George's Day on the 23rd April.

Saint George's Channel, between Ireland and Wales, Saint George's Fields, Saint George's Cathedral?

Father Doyle watched many carriages pass through the main gates of Lambeth Palace and an ironic smile appeared on his features.

The Protestant English gentry resented the Catholic success of St George's Cathedral which, when all is said and done, was partly his creation and inspiration.

It was considered an honour to receive an invitation to the garden party. He knew the guests would sit at a few separate tables and be served with lemon tea and patisserie. Father Doyle gazed at the flowers; he could see apple trees, magnolias and camellias.

He always loved the Camellia Terrace and the acres of land at Claremont House, where he spent many hours with the Royalty of Europe.

It was always considered to be an honour for all the guests, even the wealthy and well-bred.

Father Doyle wandered home, thinking of births, marriages and death and life in his own diocese.

Thank God, as a priest he was never narrow-minded nor horribly judgemental.

"Kneel down, say your prayers and confess your sins."

Girls told of their sexual activities, illegitimate babies and abortions. There were many homosexuals, paedophiles and males guilty of assault and battery, rape and burglary.

Boys had been arrested and admitted stealing 500 bodies

from the burial grounds and selling them to surgeons at the local hospitals for assessment.

"Confess your sins, my friends, and you will receive absolution. Catholics, Protestants, Jews, Quakers, a Lutheran. God Bless you all if you are believers."

★★★

Anti-Semitism was rife in the nineteenth century and some outrageous acts against the Jews took place in Russia and Hungary. There was an anti-Semitic League in Germany to restrict their liberty and the Dreyfus case in France had a religious basis.

Many Jews were very wealthy; they were brilliant business men and women and could always make money. The Rothschilds were a prime example. The family came to England after great financial success on the Continent and made another fortune in this country; their expertise was obvious from 1714.

One Rothschild became a peer in 1885 and the title was inherited by his close family.

Lionel was the first Jew to be admitted to Parliament in 1858.

Benjamin Disraeli was the grandson of a Venetian Jew; he converted from Judaism to the Church of England to ensure his political future.

It was a clever move that gave him the chance of a seat in the House of Commons.

"Dizzy" may have been heterosexual? Rumour had it that he was seen on the streets of London dressed as a lady.

He wanted to reform the country's way of life, work for the poor and needy and achieve limited working hours.

Disraeli was a very ambitious man. He never went to public school or university and began his working life as a writer. In 1842, when he was twenty-two, he wrote *Vivian Grey* and it became the talk of the town. Many admired his wit and intelligence.

After election as a Member of Parliament, Disraeli became Prime Minister, for the first time, in 1867.

He appears to have said, "Yes, I have climbed to the top of the greasy pole."

Gladstone was in the opposition, yet he was devoted to the problems of Ireland.

Dizzy became close to Queen Victoria and wrote her a letter detailing the ideal life between Her Majesty and her ministers. "On her part perfect confidence, on his perfect devotion."

Disraeli became Prime Minister for the second time in 1874. He was rewarded by the Queen and created the 1st Earl of Beaconsfield, and took his seat in the House of Lords.

He had married a very wealthy woman, the widow of Wyndham Lewis, and enjoyed a life of luxury.

It is strange to remember that many Members of Parliament shouted down his maiden speech.

Disraeli's second book, *Sybil*, clarifies his attitude to poverty. He saw the world in two classes, the rich and the poor.

London was the largest city in the world with enormous numbers of the poverty-stricken, many sleeping on filthy straw.

The wealthy lived in another world.

There were many London clubs, including The University and The Athenaeum, a great favourite with the artistic intellectuals. Many were sexually omnivorous and the opium trade had boomed.

A joke in London clubs was, "Kindly remove the General. He's been dead for three days."

According to the *Orthodox Journal*: "No Catholic should cease to contribute till he sees the spire surmount the tower, and the cock (emblem of St Peter's fall), the cross, that all within sight, from the Surrey Hill to Hampstead, and from Greenwich to Harrow may be warned that, unless they watch and pray, they will be sure to fall into temptation."

Father Doyle wrote one of his letters, describing the state of the parish: "This locality is the worst, most squalid and ragged of the borough. Taken with all its ramifications of alleys and twists.

By the time they have finished their daily toil, it requires more than common energy to take their turn on the stairs of the Priest's House, and wait one or two, perhaps three or four hours before they can make their confessions. Mass is now said every morning in the temporary schoolroom (in Webb Street), which was until lately a dissecting room, and a receptacle for stolen dead bodies.

"Numbers of persons have sought for absolution who have not attended to their duties for thirty, forty, fifty, sixty – nay, seventy-five years."

Father Doyle wrote, when he was announcing the opening of St George's as a church, "I don't like balderdash, nor prim mouths, nor sighing, nor dying, nor 'dear me! nor lack-a-day! And all about nothing. Sigh and turn up your whites, and look as you like, my dear, when you are alone, but don't make yourself mighty nincompoopish before others.

"'I don't care for nobody if nobody cares for I.' Stupid to say the best of it, but the man who said it was less of a fool than you think."

Later the priest inserted in his comments: "Latin and Greek are qualifications for a man, but brains are better, at least for this matter-of-fact kind of age."

He even refers to his own "sweet temper", in a satirical fashion.

★★★

Danny Kelly found a heap of paperwork in the drawer of an old writing-table.

A large brown envelope was addressed to "Daniel Kelly Esquire, the Great Grandson by marriage I have never met." The boy slit it open carefully with a kitchen knife; it might contain something of value to the families.

"Friend of my heart. I shall be gone to another world when you read this letter.

I know we are all striving for a free Ireland and you will fight with the liberators.

I have committed many sins as an anarchist but I bequeath all my dreams to you.

Search in the beams in the roof of the cabin and you will find the tools of my trade.

A shot gun, a sharp knife and enough petrol to light a bomb and set fire to the vice-regal home or Kilmainham Gaol. Use everything as you please to achieve the Celtic ambition.

May we be free after hundreds of years.

My love to you all. God Bless,

Liam O'Hara"

Daniel dare not show the letter to his wife, but when she was putting the kids to bed he climbed up the wooden staircase to search for the weapons. He found an old leather case, carried it down and crept out of the door and on to the strand.

God knows, he believed in every word of Liam's but he could never be a murderer. He would fight for the cause as a soldier any day.

Danny opened the dusty old bag and found the weapons.

He drowned them in water from the harbour, dug a deep hole in the shingle and buried the old man's treasures.

They were never seen again.

He said one last prayer for Liam O'Hara who might be watching him from the Heavens.

Now it was time for tea and more bedtime stories with the little ones.

Teresa said, "I know Mother and Father came here before they moved to Southwark."

Danny replied, "Thank God the Liffey doesn't stink like the Thames. That's revolting. I wonder why the water here is so clean."

"I think fresh water flows down from the mountains."

She changed the subject.

"Granddad had two sons but one was killed fighting for a free Ireland. I think he was shot down on the street by an English soldier. We are so lucky. I often wonder why we inherited the house instead of Daddy."

"I expect the old boy knew that your daddy had settled in his new home and you had the twins."

The two young lovers sat, hand in hand, gazing out of a window at the river and the golden sands.

"Let's take the kids for a party on the strand tomorrow."

"I think that is a lovely idea."

He stroked her paws.

"Granddad had the crazy idea that I might need a nanny to help me with the children. I am quite able to cope, unless we have a dozen like some of my friends."

Danny laughed. "I will try to avoid that for your sake, darling."

He kissed her. "Let's go to bed and make love now."

Nine months later there were three little Kellys.

"Did you learn maths at school?"

"Why, darling?"

"I think you must learn to subtract, not multiply."

"That's cheeky."

He kissed her gently on the lips.

"I might become a career woman like Lucia. Don't forget your brother is a devoted performer."

Old O'Hara had written to his only living son.

"The Doctors say I may only live a year so I have made a will. I leave my money to you, pictures to Stanislaus and my piano to Teresa. I think Angelina will enjoy my books. I know you are determined to stay in England. God knows why! We thought you were on board a coffin ship but a horse and dray landed you in Southwark, not the U.S.A.

I leave my ornaments, furniture and cottage to Danny Kelly and Teresa and the brood I am sure they will raise.

Remember, dockers are never short of work on the River Liffey in Dublin.

God bless you all.

Father Liam"

★★★

The Catholics of Southwark loved Father Doyle. Many were young and living in Ireland when he created the beautiful St George's in 1850.

They might not remember the days of his success, yet they admired his determination and love of the people.

For years and years his life was down to earth, not pie in the sky.

Many citizens were born long after his achievement with bricks and mortar, yet he found the time to struggle on behalf of the sick and poverty-stricken.

He could never understand the cruelty of the wealthy English gentry.

Read any penny paper and you can find and learn the facts of life – love, sex and senility.

There were new schools in South London for 500 boys and girls. They might have remained ignorant little sods, unable to read and write.

The working class – the great unwashed.

One aristo said, "There are seven classes of man, from royalty downwards. We should take advantage and employ more and more servants to work for us, in the kitchen and in the fields."

Many achieved their aim for a few pence a week.

In 1842, *The Illustrated London News* had informed the public, when writing about St George's: "The Catholics are at last stirring themselves to provide a better order of things. The report that the Pope of Rome has largely contributed to the erection of this edifice is, we hear, totally without foundation. The church has been built, in reality, by the pence of the poor."

There were write-ups in the *Anglican Ecclesiologist*, and *The Gentleman's Magazine*.

The builders were paid in instalments of £500, until the building was completed.

"There ne'er was a sight so sadly fair."

By December 1843 the house and church had been roofed.

Mr Lucas, the Editor of *The Tablet* wrote: "They say you are an odd fish, Father Doyle."

The Father was often satirical in his many letters to the Catholic weekly.

Once he wrote: "My honoured Sirs, and stately dames, and chattering school-girls, and most fatiguing blue-stockings, for your life spare your pity over Father Thomas. Anything but pity, dear things: do not now, do not pity him, for he will surely die if you be so cruel.

"What a pity! Yes indeed, what a pity!

"Truly, sadly piteous, that the Catholics of England should drive the man who under Heaven has raised the noble Church of St George to its present height, and made it Catholic property for ever, to write as he does.

Pity that some chattering and censorious Catholics should do nothing more for the great work than this – to pity Father Thomas, and ridicule him for his letters."

In another part of his correspondence he wrote: "Why denounce him as a *'scandalum datum'*, which means a scavenger?"

Bizarre

A little cock robin danced along the waterfront and into the Kelly's yard.

Hoppity-hop! Hoppity-hop!

Was he looking for food or a mate?

A rook swooped down to kill him but flew away when he saw Felix squatting nearby, reading a copy of the local rag. Sometimes his manager gave him old copies of *Punch* and *The Era*.

Maria called out from the doorway, "I have made the tea, Felix. Are you coming in or do you want a breath of fresh air?"

Felix replied: "There's a lovely robin in the yard. You must come out and have a look at him. The colour of his breast is almost cerise."

The sun was rising; it was the break of day.

"I am making bread and milk for Dad. Do you want any left-overs?"

"Yes please, Mum. I am not putting on weight. I dare not dance across the stage weighing a ton – looking like a balloon."

Jonathan called out, "It is nearly time for school. Come on, you lot."

"I picked some wild blackberries down by the river and they are as sweet as sugar. An apple fell over the wall at Lambeth Palace. It was lying on the ground so I have cooked that too."

"I'm coming now, it sounds great for breakfast."

Felix hopped towards the door.

"I am a cock robin."

Jonathan said, "I think you are a bloody idiot, lad. We have bred four guttersnipes in the family."

"Perhaps you should say we have become a family of six, Dad? A snipe is a kind of bird. I looked him up in the old dictionary. They have long, aquiline beaks. The book says the common ones are about ten inches long, with mottled brown and black feathers."

Maria butted in. "I can promise you won't get one for breakfast." They all roared with laughter.

Someone who escaped the scaffold was Oscar Wilde. He was a married man with children but, when his case came to court, he was convicted of immoral behaviour and his wife chose to use her maiden name, Holland.

The Marquess of Queensberry had chosen to report his son Bosie's relationship, with Wilde, to the police. This appears to be a strange decision as his main interest in life was boxing, in which area he was quite influential.

After two years hard labour in an English gaol, Oscar left this country and spent the rest of his life in Montmartre, on the left bank of the Seine.

Poor Oscar, a brilliant man, died when he was only forty-four years of age.

After a short while he became estranged from his young lover, Bosie.

You know Paris was the home of decadence in the music halls, the cabarets and the brothels. You could satisfy your lust for a few francs.

Oscar's parents are said to have dressed him as a pretty little girl when he was about four years of age. Their little princess! Poor boy. It may have been misleading?

"I saw a monkey in the trees with brown curly hair and a flat face", said Felix.

He had been persuaded to work in Montmartre, on the left bank of the Seine.

Stanislaus was learning all the time. Many artists and writers were sure the two young men were lovers and this was a safety net. They spent three weeks in Paris, far away from the "molly-houses", determined to return to the good life in Southwark with Father Doyle as their mentor.

Many Parisian nightclubs had mirror walls – customers could watch the sexual antics of others.

Come – Come – Come.

"I don't always understand every word you say, Stanni."

"A poet wrote 'Great minds are very near to madness."

They spent a fabulous time together. Felix said, "I am a bloody idiot, but at least I can roll my rs."

They brought home two love birds and a canary from an open market and a little money Felix had been able to save for the first time in his life.

"I never knew Le Moulin Rouge was a mill the owners had painted red. I think it is a fantastic idea that people will never forget."

"The say Prince Edward came over to Paris for the opening night."

Many Parisians adored Felix, the "song and dance" boy. Was it the act they admired or did they want to leap into bed with him after the show?

The concierge at their small hotel was sure they were an affaire. He gave them a naughty wink every night after the show.

Thank God, the two boys were good Catholics who did not end up in a male brothel, earning a small fortune.

"It's so different from the wilds of Southwark. Lords and ladies with salons for the art world. It has been a very happy journey, thank you, Stanni, for being my chaperon.

"Last night a man tried to pick me up in a pavement café near the Champs Elysees. He waved a few francs in the air but went crazy when I dumped them in the grouts of my black coffee."

★★★

Le Vicomte's pretty little boy had said, "May I use your Christian name or shall I call you Papa?"

He gave Le Vicomte a sweet smile.

"My own Daddy taught me some funny tricks, but he died of the siffi when I was only six years old. Mummy was an old bag. She always said, 'Do what the Hell you like', then dumped me and ran off with a mill hand.

Le Vicomte smiled down at the lad.

"You may call me whatever you choose. My real name is Alphonse – Alphonse Cartier. You know I have christened you Goldilocks, because of your curley-wurleys."

Marcel, the manservant, was becoming sick to death of all the decadence and decided it was time to report his master to the Metropolitan Police.

One afternoon the lovers were having a kiss and a cuddle and a little grope on the tester bed, when the door burst open.

A policeman and two army officers looked down at their naked bodies.

"I arrest you in the name of the law. I shall take you both into custody and you will face a charge of immoral behaviour. You know that is a grave offence in this country."

Tommy Goldilocks screamed. Alphonse Cartier said, "How on earth did you break into my house?"

"Perhaps your manservant omitted to lock the main doors. We already had reasons to be suspicious. Come with us. We are on the way to Newgate Prison or Horsemonger's Gaol.

The authorities will confirm one or the other. You will consort with criminals who have committed similar offences, also rape, murder and burglary."

Poor little Tommy Goldilocks was terrified, cowering under a blanket at the end of the bed.

Alphonse picked up a knife that lay in its sheath on a bedside table. He laughed, flourishing it in the air.

The three other men were en garde, but instead of trying to disembowel his bitter enemies he flung it out of the open window. It clattered on the stones, narrowly missing a baby in its mother's arms.

"Give me time to dress and I shall be ready to meet my God and the London judges, not in that order."

Le Vicomte had reached for his bag of cosmetics and taken out a pale pink rouge.

"I will make you look prettier than ever to enchant the audience."

He dabbed a little colour on the boy's rose-bud mouth and cheeks.

Tommy had been as white as a sheet, clinging to his Master's fine coat-tails.

A crowd gathered on the street, outside Alphonse Le Vicomte's house.

One yobbo shouted "They've nicked the filthy old bugger at last."

A long file of costermongers followed the vehicle on its way to gaol.

Someone sent a balloon up into the sky. An old man shouted, "The bears and the bulls and the cocks will be having a party in Heaven to celebrate the bloody man's downfall."

A woman wept into a torn rag murmuring, "I've been there when I was a child."

Someone began to chant. "Lee Viiiiscount. Lee Viiiiscount."

Foreign accents from the immigrants, Irish brogue, Cockney slang.

They arrived at their destination and were led by handcuffs into prison.

"Be brave, little one. These bastards must never know we are frightened of them. *On y va!*"

Marcel remained in the house, ashamed of his involvement.

He had been disloyal to the Master, yet the alternative would have been an ongoing life with a paedophile harming innocent little children – boys and girls.

Would his actions lead to hard labour or death on the gallows?

Perhaps Rosa Kelly would act as a witness in a court of law?

Horsemonger's Gaol

It was a bronze autumn day with scum floating on the alleyways and the river.

Stanislaus, Felix and Rosa carried paper bags full of pies, buns and lemonade for a picnic near Lambeth Palace. They were swept along by a vast crowd of mill hands, stable lads, rogues and vagabonds, and toffs from the nearby pubs and brothels.

Stanni was the only one with a few coppers to spare for a party in the open air.

Halt.

Thousands of spectators gathered at the foot of Horsemonger's Gaol to watch evil men and women hang on the scaffold.

Stanislaus said, "Thousands of people treat this as a day out and take pleasure in the death scene. I think it is a foul idea."

The three Irish youngsters clung together, otherwise the little 'un might be swept away and disappear into a whorehouse.

"Blood lust."

Two policemen climbed onto the prison roof and whipped several prisoners. A cheer rose.

"Last time they killed a man and his wife, they were accused of murder but later proved innocent. The crime may be sodomy or the rape of women and children. Boys and girls."

Rosa looked up at the sky and focused on the gallows.

"Oh Lordy, Lordy! It's my penny man. I never saw him again."

The serpentine sadist, Le Vicomte de Southwark, gazed down at the crowd below, laughed and tried to wave a hand.

Goldilocks, the little blond lad with the sky-blue eyes, hung beside him, in floods of tears.

A pretty young policeman had gathered evidence by pretending to be 'one of the girls' and sold them drugs, absinthe, laudanum and cocaine. His report contained many sexual details.

The strict Protestants proved a charge of immoral behaviour, leading to death on the gallows.

Accommodation for the sightseers was as melancholy as the black beams above.

Two black silhouettes appeared at the head of the scaffold. One was tall and slim, the other short and plump.

The agony of death fouled the man's body.

The coarse rope snapped the tender bones at the nape of the boy's neck.

They hung like slaughtered pigs in the abattoir.

Le Vicomte's world of passion, love and sex was over. Books and art, lashings of money, life in Mayfair with the aristos and Southwark with the bulls and bears and cocks.

Cock-a-doodle-do!

He had tried to wave at little Rosa but his hands were tied.

His life had come to an end.

Pray God, his early belief was true. There was another life, in Purgatory, Heaven or Hell.

Now he fell through the trap doors beneath his feet, saying his prayers.

The crowd of onlookers booed and cheered. Blood lust. That's entertainment!

Rosa was crying her eyes out for the poor old man who had been so kind to her.

Love and kisses from a serpent.

She turned away from the gallows, stumbling through the muddy grass.

A six foot man, built like a giant, knocked the little girl with his elbow and she fell, face down, into the muck and mire.

Rosa opened her mouth to scream but only swallowed rubbish from the ground.

She lay, choking. Felix and Stanislaus picked her up by the feet and shoulders.

"You can't walk, Rosa. We will carry you home."

Flossie-Bang-Bang and Tinky-Poo were resting on Rosa's tummy as she lay dying.

The child murmured, "I will see you all in Wonderland," and took her last breath of air in this world.

Maria said to Jonathan, "I want to kill myself; Rosa was always my dearest child."

"You still have three others, darling, and you are young enough to give birth again."

"God forbid any more pains in the belly and feeling as sick as a dog."

"Don't be so crude, Maria. Remember Rosa helping you when Lucia was born."

Jonathan took his wife's hand.

"Rosa is in another world, my love. Be brave. Our tragedy must be the will of God. Talk to Father Doyle, he might be able to console you."

Maria shrugged her shoulders. "How on earth can we have a wake in this hell-hole?"

"I will scrub the floor. Rosa was never an angel, but she may be floating in the air and gazing down at us. Father Doyle will be here and the O'Haras. You know Stanislaus was with the child when she fell near the gallows.

Let us say our prayers and talk no more of suicide; we both know it is a sin in the Catholic Church."

He kissed his dear wife and they sat together in silence.

At a wake people were offered a "wee wain" for the men and a small port for the ladies. With the Kellys this was likely to be tea, home-made cake and cordial. Neighbours came during the day bringing snuff, plug tobacco and clay pipes. Michael O'Hara brought a welcome barrel of beer, and Father Doyle joined the family and friends, with a few small gifts of food and drinks.

Jonathan and Felix made a coffin of driftwood from the waterfront, lay it on a worm-eaten wooden bench and lit candles at the head and foot.

It was a party with games and story-telling after midnight. The rosary was recited.

At supper-time women usually sat with the body while the men remained in the kitchen.

This would be a pauper's funeral. Some families could afford to lay ribbons and flowers on the coffin while they talked to their loved ones.

Later the grey body of the child would be lifted onto the death cart by Jonathan, Stanislaus and Felix. Father Doyle rode with the cadavers.

Maria knelt at the foot of the makeshift coffin and whispered, "Dearest Rosa, you are my own flesh and blood. May you find love and peace in Heaven." She made the sign of the cross. The child had always been at risk in this world, living in the slums of England.

Maria felt as sick as a pig after eating and drinking with the family and the O'Haras at the wake. The hovel was silent as a grave. Jonathan helped his wife to her feet.

Rosa might be longing to call out a last message to her family and friends. Her mother looked up at the large, fluffy white clouds scudding across the sky and imagined an angel floating on the bare branches of a weeping willow near the river.

A peel of laughter rang out and a light voice called, "Rosa! Rosa in Wonderland! You always said, 'You must not moan if anything strange or horrible seems to be happening to me. I shall be like the animals down the rabbit hole in *Alice in Wonderland*.'"

It was the voice of young Annie, the girl's best friend at school. She had been regaled with so many stories about the family history of the Kellys, good and bad.

Silence. Deathly silence, broken by one of the men.

Three hundred cadavers lay on the death cart and Father Doyle was not afraid to ride with them to the burial ground. So many were terrified of the cholera, but he knew his faith in God would protect him.

Some mourners followed the bodies of their loved ones on foot. A few were praying for divine intervention but it was far too late.

The government tried to insist that all bodies should be buried within twelve days of their departure from this world.

Felix had sung in Gaelic at the wake, a tribute to his little sister and her new life in Heaven, "Ave Maria". Stanislaus followed the horse and dray on foot. "I am so sorry, Mrs Kelly, Rosa was a lovely child. We became very close after my sister's wedding."

He picked a bunch of wild flowers from the roadside and flung it on the cart. Tears flowed.

Stanislaus was eighteen.

He wanted to paint a portrait of Rosa, a gift for her mother, Maria. He was sure she would hang it on a wall of their hovel.

A pink rose would be escapist.

Auburn hair, pale ivory skin and sparkling blue eyes.

Stanislaus had never painted a human being, only animals. Rabbits, stray dogs and cats, chameleons that changed colour and snapped their tails.

He chose a small canvas from his shop and began the portrait. It was diabolical.

Now he chose to paint the little girl in profile. A cloud of curly hair, a retroussé nose, a black outline of her thick eyelashes.

Stanislaus had another idea; he would paint a black and white pussy cat in the child's arms; she had told him her story of Le Vicomte.

To Hell with the evil Marquis de Sade.

Stanislaus might have painted Rosa's bare pink bum rising in the air; he could imagine Maria's reaction.

She was in floods of tears again when he gave her the picture.

"I shall treasure it for the rest of my life."

★★★

In May 1846, the annual dinner on behalf of the Southwark Catholic Charity Schools took place with the famous Daniel O'Donnell in the chair.

H. Robinson Esq. proposed a toast: "To the memory of two Right Rev. Prelates, Dr Bramston and Dr Poynter, both interested in the success of these schools. While I call your attention to the memory of the dead," he continued, "I cannot refrain from bestowing the well-earned meed of praise on the living, energetic, zealous successor therein of these admirable men – Dr Doyle, whose exertions in the cause of the noble Cathedral of St George are so well known.

"It would seem a kind of retribution that the noble Catholic structure should rise on the very spot where Lord George Gordon assembled his lunatic mob and urged them on to their work of devastation and plunder of the Catholics."

★★★

The Father's tummy rumbled like a drum. He was losing weight, walking miles and skipping meals to save money for the cause. Soon he would be as thin as a rake with a nose like a parrot's beak or a sharp sword. He was longing for another meal at Claremont – seven fantastic courses! Beef, pork or lamb, pot-au-feu, profiteroles, meringues, strawberry fool. Petit fours.

One lady had written about the house and its "elegant rusticity".

Father Thomas wanted to see the gardens again, the peacocks, and the Camellia Terrace.

He sat at his desk to write his usual witty weekly letter to *The Tablet*, the Catholic paper, and, within minutes, he was fast asleep.

Young Victoria wrote about Claremont describing her young life there. "The happiest days of my otherwise dull childhood."

Leopold admitted to friends that he could not bear to live in Claremont without his beloved wife.

"St George's Fields are no more,
The trowel supersedes the plough.
Huge inundated swamps of grass
Are changed to civic villas now."

Miss Mary, a young Brighton lady, begs the Father "to accept the enclosed Post Office order for five pounds which my Papa has given me as a birthday present. I cannot think of any present more acceptable than the protection of Our Blessed Lady."

On 6th January 1846, Father Doyle was able to announce good news about St George's Church.

There is a melange of reaction from many quarters, yet there is a feeling of pity expressed for him.

"Has he called anyone by a bad name? Or told thumpers? Or given thumps? Or violently taken away a man of woman's money? If he has charmed away the gold from the rich pocket, and by the black art withdrawn the costly diamond earrings, or rich stomacher of pearls? What is that to you, Mrs Evil-Eye, and Mr Pomposity Hold-fast?"

Victoria and Albert relaxed from their Royal duties, even walking together, without bodyguards, on the Brighton Palace Pier. Life on the Isle of Wight was more conventional; all the children wanted was to play games in the gardens.

The attitude of the Royal Yacht Club based in Cowes was rigid; they refused to accept Prince Albert because he was a foreigner. His wife built him a house of his own so he could sail in peace without interference from the bigots.

Queen Victoria said to one of her ladies-in-waiting, "You know we spent little more than an hour on our journey from London to Brighton."

Her Royal Highness always preferred her beloved Osborne House on the Isle of Wight to the Royal Pavilion, but she enjoyed her travels.

She always thought the elaborate dragon light in the ceiling of one reception room in the Royal Pavilion was sinister.

Victoria was aware of the love story between the Roman Catholic, Mrs Fitzherbert, and the Prince Regent. Rumour said there was a tunnel between his exotic Oriental residence and her home on the Old Steyne, but the Queen preferred to ignore this information.

"They say George Stephenson's Rocket Train travels at thrity-five miles an hour, it flashes like lightning."

★★★

Stanislaus took Felix to Brighton as a birthday treat, with a lecture about the old Brighthelmstone en route. They strolled along the Palace Pier and the Promenade. A few male day-trippers were "working the rail"; slang for "on the pick-up".

The sea-front and the squares were lined with beautiful regency houses. One day, maybe?

Stanislaus might paint shrimps and raw black lobsters, scallops, starfish and an octopus?

"Stanni, Stanni! I've bought you a crab to paint in your studio."

They gobbled up fish and chips from old newspapers and toddled home with happy hearts and full tummies.

★★★

Father Doyle asked one of the worshippers in St George's Cathedral, "Have you met Dr Barnardo? They tell me he is working very hard to help the poverty-stricken in the East End. He came over from Dublin in 1866 intending to study at the London Hospital in Stepney and became a medical missionary.

"Dr Barnardo soon established his first home and shelter for the young, with the use of an old stable. Since then he has established many, many more.

"They tell me thousands of young people are trained and emigrate to Canada. I suppose they travel from Tilbury Docks. It would be another world for them, another life.

"They say he is building a church especially for children.

He must be a beggar, like me. Tell me, is this fine man Catholic or Protestant?"

"I have no idea. He is another Thomas, Thomas John Barnardo, born 1845. He did evangelistic work in the slums of Dublin before crossing the Irish Sea."

One of the younger men said, "I know a few details about Dr Barnardo because my family live in Stepney. He went to St Patrick's Grammar School and became one of the Plymouth Brethren like his mother and sisters. You know how strict they are, Father. They don't believe in ordination and celebrate the Lord's Supper every Sunday.

"We are all trying to help the poor children in so many ways. Dr Barnardo will accept any creed but he separates them. If possible Jewish children are handed to the Jewish Board of Guardians in London and Roman Catholics to their own institutions."

The Father said, "I am amazed he is so judgemental."

"Dr Barnardo is one of seventeen children and I think his upbringing may have been a little tough."

"His idea of building a church for children is fantastic. His work is fabulous but I fear we would have little in common from a religious angle."

Corn And Potatoes

In 1804 many new restrictions, including the Corn Laws, had been imposed on exports and imports at the London Corn Exchange.

The import of cheap grain was banned. The price of home wheat had been fixed at fifty shillings a quarter. It rose to sixty-six shillings. A four pound loaf of bread now cost a shilling, not eight pence. This caused great hardship for the poor. There were many land enclosures and small "strip farmers" sold their land at low prices.

In 1838 the price of corn continued to rise but there was hope of reform. This was promoted by Robert Peel but opposed by many Tories. The aristocratic government, supported by Disraeli and the Duke of Wellington, wished for total control.

The poverty-stricken Irish tried to grow their own potatoes in old wooden boxes, dreading the blight.

Duties on maize were abolished in 1846; wheat, oats and barley taxes would be scrapped, in the meantime they were reduced to a shilling a quarter.

Peel hoped this would help the growing population. Starving peasants still clamoured for food at the gates of an Irish workhouse.

There was cheaper shipping after 1850, by sail and steam boats. Modern agricultural machinery was coming into use.

Prairie farms in North America produced vast quantities of corn. Peasant farms in the Russian Empire had cheap labour.

Every country increased tariffs except Britain and Belgium.

Many agricultural labourers relocated to the cities and found other work; some small grain farmers emigrated.

Cereal production was labour intensive in Ireland.

The political power of the middle class increased throughout the century.

★★★

Stanislaus told his father, "I am moving to a studio close to the river at World's End, Chelsea. It is near the harbour and there is a coterie of artists. I love the name. I should be in my element."

Michael said, "I shall miss you, boy. Your little shop, Fur and Feathers, was quite close to us but we could have built you a studio shed in the garden."

"I want to be independent, Dad. You know I'm quite ambitious with some of my naturalistic paintings. Some families live in a barge on the Thames. They try to be grand and call them house-boats. I would never risk it. Any kids or animals might fall overboard and drown in the water."

"They tell me it has become fashionable to plant gardens in the front of houses instead of rearing sheep and cattle. We could be very la-de-dah with a studio at the rear of the villa."

"Thanks, Dad. It is a great offer, but no thanks."

A horse and carriage moved Stanislaus to his new abode with his easel, canvases, paints and brushes. He became wildly extravagant and bought a new tester bed, dining table, chairs and chaise longue. It was cheaper than transport might have been.

Flowers and wild animals would replace the Fur and Feathers.

Cream paint decorated the walls and another lodger had left a pair of pale green chintz curtains printed with yellow rosebuds.

Some of his own pictures would embellish the apartment.

Stanislaus had acquired his own "digs" at last – kitchen, bathroom, bed-sitter and studio.

He asked the caretaker to find him a charlady to keep the rooms clean. There was not time to waste on household chores.

After a few weeks he would be happy to meet some of the other artists living in the neighbourhood. He knew that one Bohemian often woke late after binge-drinking, put on his trilby hat and bolted to the nearest tavern in his nightshirt. This behaviour was acceptable in Chelsea.

The caretaker warned Stanislaus, "Beware of the bad lads, Sir. They play tricks on our lodgers. Their latest game is to block the main door to an apartment from outside with bricks or metal bars. Then they light old newspapers soaked in petrol and shove them through the letter box. The tenant cannot escape; one fell on his rump and died."

"Thanks for warning me. Don't worry; I shall be able to cope."

Stanislaus did a brilliant job after keeping a bucket of water to pour on the flames and squirting the boys with piss from the privy pail.

"The silly sods might set fire to the building."

The caretaker said, "The charwoman will be with you tomorrow, Sir, about eleven o'clock."

A loud knock came on the door. Stanislaus was amazed to see his old tinker friend once again.

The crone emerged from the shadows. "I have brought you a gift, my friend."

She offered him a red rose wrapped in an Irish flag and

disappeared into the night for the second time in his life. Would she appear whenever he faced a serious decision?

Thank God, sex had never been a problem. He did not fancy men or women, children or animals. He was far too ambitious and would never forget his love of art. One day he might marry and have children but he imagined that was all far away in the future.

For a brief moment he remembered that dirty old man, Le Vicomte, hung on the gallows at Horsemonger's Gaol for his immoral behaviour. Tears flooded his eyes, thinking of Rosa and their stories by the riverside; *Alice in Wonderland* and the little girl falling down the rabbit hole. He said prayers for the child every year on the anniversary of her death.

Sometimes Stanislaus had romantic dreams of love, a wife and children.

Three weeks later the tinker lady reappeared saying, "You are my friend. I have shadowed you from Southwark to the World's End. My son brought one of his horses and towed my caravan to Chelsea Harbour. Now we are closer than ever, young man."

"I have sold several of my pictures and I would like a barge on the river, but it would be a lonely life." He beamed at the tinker lady. "Perhaps it is time for me to fall in love and marry?"

"I know, young Sir, I know."

"Can you suggest any lovely young lady living in Chelsea?"

"There is a darling, innocent little Tinker girl. She is seventeen years old and as pretty as a picture. If you were to marry in Ireland many receptions are held on the beach at Youghal. The police ignore the ceremony till midnight when all the tinkers have escaped and the strand is empty."

"That sounds wonderfully romantic. Where could we meet?"

"She is staying with me in the caravan, so I could arrange it. Her name is Virginia." The tinker lady chuckled. "I think it would be a wonderful marriage. Now I will tell you a secret. Virginia is my granddaughter. You would become my beloved grandson-in-law."

> *"All things bright and beautiful,*
> *All creatures great and small.*
> *All things bright and beautiful",*
> *The good Lord loves them all.*

Someone dying said, "I would give up ten thousand lives for my God."

★★★

Stanislaus was instructing his reluctant pupil, Felix, with lessons in Fine Art.

"I expect you have heard of the Impressionist Movement and the artist, Berthe Morisot? She was born in France in 1841, married a naval officer and lived in Montmartre. Edouard Manet became her brother-in-law and this opened a new world of creativity. Dozens of women began to work in art and politics.

There is an American woman, Georgia O'Keefe, who is obsessed with female genitalia: sex, abuse, and glamour. The French government has a few strange ideas about money. Every baby, legitimate or a bastard, receives francs at birth.

If you find a painting by Renoir it might fetch twenty million."

Stanislaus told Felix, "Voltaire wanted actors in his plays to have "devils in their bodies". In this century people talk about the romantic, boulevard, bourgeois theatre.

Subtile et fade, sentimentale.

You know I am dedicated to art of any kind: painting, sculpture, acting.

Many actors lack imagination and only want to project their own personalities; sod the characters they are playing. Thank the Lord that does not apply to the music hall. You are as free as air and may become a star, beloved of the English, Irish and even the Americans. Go for it, boy. I will do anything I can to help you. I can see you marching along Broadway in a top hat and tails."

"Now you are going too far, Stanislaus. I might be a poor old bugger, in rags, cowering under St George's waiting to be carried away to the workhouse."

"Not in a million years, boy. I would take a bet on that. I might even try to rescue you myself."

★★★

Maria threw a note into the harbour.

Years ago she had found a bottle on the strand in Waterford. A letter was written in fine italic script.

> *"Dear Maria,*
>
> *I regret to say this is not a proposal of marriage. I am a merchant seaman working on my Father's ship. I am married, with a happy wife and three children, two boys and a girl.*
>
> *I am an Italian Catholic, wishing you a man and babies in the near future.*
>
> *Written with a loving heart,*
> *Pablo*
> *You must escape from life near the ferry crossing. There are many bad eggs around.*   *X"*

The young girl was delighted with the swift riposte to her letter in a bottle. She showed it to Grandma Canty, to keep her in the picture.

That evening Maria took the two mongrel dogs for a walk on the lane beneath the hills. Suddenly they barked like crazy. A donkey cart had lost a wheel and overturned in the middle of the road. A tall, handsome young man strode towards her.

"I am so sorry, there are crates everywhere blocking your passage. I will go home and beg my father to give me a hand. I have begun work at the English aristo's house on the hill".

Maria laughed. "That is very strange. I am one of the scullery maids."

"How old are you, little one?"

"I am fifteen, coming up sixteen."

The little girl stroked the donkey's muzzle. He was grazing by the wayside. "I would like to live with you."

The boy, Jonathan, laughed saying, "We might arrange that one day."

They were married in the little local church and emigrated to England, scarpering across Waterford Harbour on a ferry boat.

★★★

Stanislaus found two oil paintings on the open market in Bermondsey.

The portrait of a young woman resembled Queen Victoria. She wore a white gown with bare shoulders and an emerald drape. The other picture was a landscape – *Beyond the Pale*. Someone had written the three words in italics on the back of the frame.

They might both be Irish? He knew *Beyond the Pale* meant over the border that separated the native Irish from the English invaders in Dublin.

They were both dirty and covered in dark grey dust. The portrait was filthy. He rubbed them gently with half a potato and cleaned off the sticky rubbish with a soft cloth. Now he could see grass, trees and a pale blue sky with a low church in the background.

How on earth did these lovely pictures arrive on the street in South London? Should he report them to the police, treasure them in his studio, or sell them in an auction house that could trace their history?

A collector like Rothschild or the Earl of Carnarvon might buy them for a fortune.

At last he would be free to travel the world like Father Doyle and visit the art galleries in Paris, Berlin and Munich.

There was a knock on his studio door in World's End and his old Romany tinker friend appeared yet another time in his life.

"Good evening, my dear. You will remember I predicted your success in many different areas. I have been watching over your career from a distance. Perhaps I was meant to be your Grandmother." She laughed; a low, musical cackle.

"Do not worry; I am not here to scrounge any gifts or money, only to reassure you. I saw you buy two pictures on the open market. There will not be any problems with their origin. I know the owners sold them for a few coppers when they were desperately short of money. Do not weep for these English men. They had ponced on the Irish and the tinkers long enough."

The tinker lady had a long black pigtail draped over one shoulder. She was crowned by a large pink flower resting on white lace sepals.

"My name is Anastacia. I am fifty-five years of age, young Sir."

She murmured a little nursery rhyme about the sparrow who killed the cock robin.

"I was living with my parents, 'beyond the pale', in Ireland. I am sure you know that divides the native Irish from their English lords and masters. They say about 80% of land is controlled by the invaders. They are as fat as pigs, gutzing on the farmers' money.

"I might live in my caravan by the riverside until I die, or scarper back to be in the South, near Cork. My dear husband was shot down in the street by a soldier. Thank God, our children survive, but I will not ponce on them for food and drink. I can earn enough pennies to survive with my needlework and a little cooking in the pubs and the whorehouses. I will leave you now, and many thanks for your kindness."

Stanislaus bowed. "You are more than welcome."

"There is a giant spider on the floor, Sir. They are lucky. I will wrap him up in my yellow scarf and free him by the riverside. Good night again, I will return very soon."

She ambled away down the cinder path and faded into the night.

Several weeks later she paid the young man another visit.

"My little innocent is longing to meet her fiancé, Stanislaus, for the first time in her life. She fell in love with your little portrait; it is sitting above my camp bed.

"If you marry on the strand in Youghal the family will club together and buy you a gypsy caravan. Then, for every baby in your life there will be a gift of Waterford glass from the travellers."

"My dear Anastacia, you are jumping the gun. We have not even met one another."

"I have every confidence, young Sir. The little one is my granddaughter, you will be my grandson."

★★★

Father Doyle and Lucia Kelly were sitting, side by side, on a bench near the River Thames.

The little one was at ease talking to the priest about her hopes and dreams.

Lucia said, "I don't want to lead a normal female life when I grow older. So many women marry and have a brood of kids. They spend the rest of their life washing nappies, cooking and scrubbing wooden floors."

"You have been watching your Mummy Maria and her friends."

"That way of life would drive me crazy; I know it brings joy to many people. My great ambition is to be a teacher, in an English Poor School or abroad. I have heard stories about a woman called Annie Besant. They say she believes women should be free to choose their own way of life."

"You might even marry an aristocratic gentleman for money."

Lucia laughed. "What a foul idea for a priest, Father. Mother says we marry for love. I want to go to a university, but I know that very few will accept girl students."

"I think there are three with special colleges. Oxford, Cambridge and London."

"Thank you, Father. Now I know where I want to go and I will work hard to pass all my exams. Please don't tell Mum and Dad. I want it to be our little secret."

★★★

There was a litter bin outside the back door of Stanni's apartment house. One night he bent down to deposit his rubbish. Pale gold flashed in the evening light.

Stanislaus leaned forward to retrieve something from the bin; it might be any old thing.

He saw an antique bracelet of pure gold with a design of two dragons' heads. Should he donate it to the council as part of the local heritage or sell it at one of the auction houses? Sotheby's in New Bond Street or Christie's?

On the day of the auction Stanislaus sat with the bidders and waited and waited for his lot to be raised in the air by one of the porters.

One hundred pounds. Two hundred pounds. The price rose, higher and higher.

The young man had made a fortune, out of the rubbish bin.

This was not a matter of skill or artistry, only the luck of the draw.

Money from an alien land, a treasure from the history of England.

Shoppers on the streets of London were buying all the little luxuries they could afford. Leeches, moustache grease and a pint of animal blood were thought to be everyday essentials but "You must have a penny to bless yourself with."

Many doctors prescribed leeches to remove bad blood and it was said to guard against tuberculosis.

Chemists sold toxic arsenic to kill vermin. Murder was becoming easier every minute of the day.

Gun merchants, tripe dressers and wax merchants selling candles were common-place.

Gin was a great favourite with boozers who could afford to spend a rash penny or two.

A fiddle, a harp and a trumpet were often played, by ear, on the street.

The Britannia saloon was converted to a music hall and the audience paid a penny each.

The Henley Regatta and the Grand National were great entertainment for the gentry from 1839.

Many costermongers were street traders and in the 1840s there were about 40,000 peddling their wares.

Hot potatoes, winkles and whelks; oysters were four a penny.

The Alhambra began life in 1854 as the Royal Panopticon but Science and the Fine Arts were too grand to attract a large public so it closed in two years.

Charles Morton bought the old Canterbury Arms, a purpose-built music hall near Westminster Bridge, the area known as Lambeth Marsh. It was squalid, but its history went back 300 years.

An amateur room, for gentlemen only, was free of charge. Some of the regular customers were servants from Buckingham Palace. The admission fee was six pence, including drinks, and the boom continued through the 1860s. Most of the performers were from eight years old to twenty.

Morton was a very ambitious man who made a small fortune from the love of his life – the theatre

★★★

A few of the wealthy residents of Southwark spent a long weekend in Brighton, the Queen of Watering Places. Queen Victoria and Prince Albert often chose a long weekend in the Royal Pavilion instead of her beloved Osborne House on the Isle of Wight. Chinoiserie was all the vogue, but it was not Her Majesty's favourite style.

★★★

Stanislaus was trying to teach Felix many things about art and culture without sounding like a professor from the Dublin University.

"The author, George Reynolds, wrote about poverty in London in the '30s and '40s. He also covered cultural life in Paris and opened a bookshop in the French capital. He always considered himself to be a smart, handsome and a young gentleman. There were so many problems in life, from cholera to abortions, yet there was a museum of Romantic Life.

"Many thought Reynolds was a good writer but not a great one. He became hooked on penny-dreadfuls, cheap and popular reading, worked in bookshops and became a radical politician.

"In many ways I think he resented Charles Dickens and his early work – *Sketches by "Boz"*. He loved to discuss the Glorious French Republic and the Mysteries of London. Surely one cannot deride a man like Dickens?

"He worked in a factory and as a boot-black boy on the streets of London when his father served a prison sentence in Newgate Gaol, for incurring debts, like Mr Micawber. Sackcloth to Ashes.

"I forgot to tell you about one of Reynolds' characters. Every night he sang La Marseillaise from beginning to end, before going to bed. I think he must have been a very strange bloke indeed.

Away with the fairies!"

★★★

Michael O'Hara lay in a hammock, ruminating about his way of life.

So many young boys and girls crave money and a title when they marry. The idea has been instilled into them by their parents.

A house in the country, an apartment in London. A horse

and chaise. Footmen, kitchen-maids, valets and ladies' maids. A life of luxury! A suite at the Savoy Hotel or Claridges.

Michael O'Hara was never greedy for his own children. They needed food and drink and a good Catholic education. Please God; they would never be waifs and strays.

When his beloved wife died he concentrated on work and their offspring, but he felt desperately lonely. Every night he knelt at the bedside and prayed to meet her again in Heaven.

He longed for a life in Paradise with the woman he loved.

Sometimes he dreamed he could see her elegant, curvaceous body strolling down the wooden staircase towards him. Michael raised his arms and whispered, "Anna."

Outsiders would consider him to be a tough, physical man, longing to sleep with any woman. They were all wrong; Anna lived on in his mind and body. Would he ever be able to love another woman, in or out of bed?

Michael was tall, dark and handsome at fifty years of age. Perhaps a second marriage could be true in a totally different way? Now the children had flown the coop and he was alone for hours on end.

An agency had provided him with a young housekeeper from overseas; housework would no longer prove to be one of his problems.

The office girl said, "I know Natasha will be happy to work in the garden and the villa. She is an excellent cook. Roast and two veg on Sundays and some more exotic dishes for the rest of the week."

The girl blushed. She had gone a bit too far when talking to this gentleman.

Now Michael lay in bed listening to the leaves of the willow tree brushing against the bedroom window.

It was a bright spring morning and Michael O'Hara was on a week's holiday. He was determined to enjoy his freedom from work, with pale ale, cups of tea, glasses of bubbly and music.

Michael and Stanislaus picked a bunch of flowers from the garden. They were pink and white, camellias and roses. They wrapped them in coloured paper, tied with a pink satin ribbon.

Together they carried the posy along the riverside until they reached Kelly's hovel.

Maria was on her hands and knees scrubbing the filthy, dark brown floorboards.

"We have brought you a few flowers, in memory of Rosa. You know we shall be thinking of you this weekend."

Maria kissed the flowers and burst into tears. The kindness of the O'Haras was overwhelming, they were good people. She mopped her eyes and flashed a weak smile.

"I think you only met my little one a few times. She was a darling child and believed she was Rosa in Wonderland who fell down a magic rabbit hole and lived with fairies and animals. Someone wrote or said 'Remember the good things in this life."

She smiled, clasping the flowers to her bosom.

Michael had been heart-broken when he lost his wife a few years ago. He could understand her feelings, with so many memories.

Maria fingered her rosary and made the Sign of the Cross.

"In the name of the Father and of the Son and of the Holy Ghost."

Another wake?

He stretched across the double four-poster bed and said, "Good night, my dearest love," before falling asleep, alone, at midnight. He often woke up in the morning cuddling the eiderdown.

The bidet in the bathroom was shrouded in light grey dust.

He mumbled to himself at five o'clock in the morning,

"Concentrate on your work, you silly sod," and dashed out of the house to the river.

The other Kellys were still around, and Father Doyle. Stanislaus was living near Chelsea.

Another girl? Another world?

One day he was weeding in the garden and chatting with Natasha. The girl was as thin as a lathe. She laughed; a low, childish gurgle. "I shall be your slave, my lord, to cook and tidy and make sure you have clean bed clothes."

"William Wilberforce abolished the slave trade years ago."

"I may be mixed-race, but I am free now to love and serve you, my lord."

That evening Natasha knelt on Michael's bedroom floor with a bowl of warm, soapy water.

She tickled the soles of his feet with her long, tapering fingers and he laughed.

"It could be dangerous to play games, my dear, but don't worry. Father Doyle would vouch for me. I am a good Catholic, I am not going to throw you on the bed and rape you."

There was a long pause. "I have been a lonesome man for some years now."

Bronze hair framed her oval face; there were light hollows under her cheekbones. Her eyes were the colour of spring violets.

Michael O'Hara smiled down at the young girl. "I am old enough to be your father, but I want to make love to you. I must explain. I could not bear to live in a friendly marriage where the most intimate relationship was a peck on the cheek and two single beds. I hope this doesn't sound crude. Please forget this offer of marriage if you find the idea of passion revolting. Don't worry, my dear, I would never give you the sack. You are doing a grand job; I would never throw you out on to the streets of London."

The girl gave him a sweet smile. "I know that, Sir. I am so happy living with you, but I am sure I would be far happier in a marriage. I love you; I think I fell in love when I walked through the door of the villa. I have never slept with a man or a woman. You will be my teacher."

"That is wonderful news, almost too good to be true. You know one of my daughters is a nun, another is married and living in Ireland. My only son, Stanislaus, is a fine artist with his own studio. Oh Lord, I have one query. What is your religion?"

"That will never be a problem; I was brought up as a Papist. You know my family died before I was shipped to England. There is one little secret. I am mixed-race, but my Father was an Irish Catholic. My real name is Natasha Donovan!"

"That is wonderful. I know Father Doyle will be happy to marry us. I think it will be a simple wedding."

Natasha crossed the room.

Michael took her hands.

There was a sweet scent of eau de cologne.

There was a long pause.

"I have been a lonesome man for several years now. Will you share my life… and marry me?"

"The answer is *Oui, Monsieur. Si, Senor.* I have loved you ever since the moment we met.

Will your three children accept a mixed-race girl in the family?"

"They are all broad-minded; there will never be any racial problems."

Michael kissed Natasha gently on the lips.

Michael said to his fiancée, "When we are married I think I shall retire as a wharfinger. I love working in the garden, I am sure we could grow all our own fruit and vegetables. We might even plan a little apple orchard. I love animals – stray cats and dogs, even some of the exotic models used by my son,

Stanislaus. Hedgehogs, chameleons and snakes. You know the young man is an artist. I loathe food like *pâté de foie gras*. The whole idea is revolting, yet some call it a gourmet's delight."

Six months later, after his own quiet second wedding, it was decided to hold a feast in the villa to celebrate the Kellys move into their new home – the Pig Sty.

Michael said, "If we do it on a grand scale they will think I am as rich as Croesus. I am sure you have heard of the famous King of Lydia who said, 'Call no man happy before his death'."

He took his wife's long, brown, tapering fingers in his square hands and whispered, "Even kings and the elite can be wrong."

They lay, clasping one another, on the soft double bed.

Natasha's meal was far more exotic than Angelina's would have been: spice and rice, pasta with salmon and chocolate éclairs.

Everyone gorged and drank a toast to the new life of the Kellys: Mum, Dad and Lucia. Stanislaus came from his new studio in Chelsea.

Angelina was living in a convent on the Isle of Jersey. She could not escape to celebrate; the Mother Superior would not release her. She rejoiced in her Father's marriage to Natasha, the mixed-race virgin. She understood how lonesome he had been after their Mother's death.

Kelly's Pig Sty

Maria was sewing a lady's skirt because the hem had become unravelled and the old girl could not see well enough to do it herself. She might trip over it and fall to the ground.

Maria finished her work and put away her needle and thread.

She gazed up at the pale blue sky: feathery white clouds fluttered in the sunlight.

God! How she longed to be back in Ireland beside the river in Waterford. This was her wild dream whenever she was alone, but she was exiled to this rookery for the rest of her life. She yearned for a log cabin on a piece of open land, with ducks and chickens and a cow to milk. Pure milk from a cow's udders not watered-down slosh.

Early that morning they had all eaten bread and milk – stale bread softened on the hob. Maria knew she was praying for the impossible.

It was time to get moving; Jonathan would soon be home for his crusty bread and dripping.

She folded the old girl's skirt; the needlework was her one good deed for the day.

Someone said, "One good deed deserves another."

Maria loved Jonathan and all the family, she would never leave them.

Perhaps they had all made the greatest mistake of their lives, fleeing Ireland after the famine. There might be a long, sordid life ahead. She and her husband were still only in their thirties.

Tomorrow she would appeal to Father Doyle for advice on how she might live without moaning and whining to herself.

It was time to confess her sins – again.

She felt there might be some excitement in the near future.

The O'Haras had planned a party on St Patrick's Day.

God Bless us all!

Maria shivered. The sun was rising, but a strong wind blew up her bum. She had a large hole in her thin blue knickers. Her one and only tattered vest lay in the litter bin; it was beyond redemption.

This morning she had emptied the privy pail down the drain but she could still smell the family's piss and pooh. It reeked in her nostrils.

Lucia had said, "I can help you, Mummy," but she was only seven years old and it was not fair to impose housework on a kid of that age.

Maria sniffed, trying to clear her nose, then mopped up the dripping liquid with the back of her hand.

Poor woman! She really enjoyed some domesticity, cleaning and cooking, but these conditions were horrible and had been so for many years.

Her second son, Felix, was doing well, but his life was spent rehearsing and performing around England, Dublin and even some of the night clubs and music halls of Paris.

He had so little time to spare for any thing or any one away from the footlights and his spotlight. Many people talked about a better life for the poor but they never seemed to achieve a great deal. Maria tied one of Jonathan's old scarves round her head as a turban and set to work on the chicken carcass, cooking for the family's high tea.

Daddy Jonathan had finished work at the pub, chopping logs for the fire on Saturday night's cockfighting. He was strutting home with three pennies in his trouser pocket.

He fancied a bun and a glass of ale but he knew the mother was in desperate need of food for their evening meals. Chitterlings or tripe, a rabbit or a cat to feed two grown-ups and Lucia. He knew there was a reeking chicken carcass in the back cupboard, but the mere thought of it made him feel sick.

Sod it. The pennies fell to the bottom of his trouser pocket; Jonathan managed to catch them before they escaped into the gutter or down the drain.

He nearly jumped out of his skin when Felix danced out of the bushes by the wayside, flourishing a large white envelope in mid-air.

"It's a little surprise present from all the O'Haras and me to celebrate your wedding anniversary. Open it now, then I can see your face when you read the small print. I promise you it's legal. God Bless you both, Daddy. Break a leg, as they say in the theatre."

Jonathan slit open the envelope and saw the name of a well-known London solicitor.

"It's too good to be true. I can't believe it."

"Every word is true, Daddy. Have a wonderful time for the next few years."

Felix blew a kiss in the air, did one of his famous somersaults and skipped away through the bushes towards the River Thames.

Jonathan came down the path, grinning like a Cheshire cat.

"I suppose you have been hitting the bottle. Are you as pissed as a newt in Paradise?"

"No way. I've got some wonderful news, Maria."

"Don't tell me Teresa is having another baby."

"No way. This affects the three of us. Come away from that little log fire or you will go up in flames."

He dowsed the burning wood with liquid from the gutter and it stank. The chicken bones lay reeking at the bottom of the pot.

Maria said, "Thank God Lucia has fallen asleep. We have only got two potatoes and this carcass for supper."

"Don't worry, darling, we shall never go hungry again."

"Have you sold your soul to the devil?"

"No way."

He sat down with a plonk, his fat bum overflowing on to the cobblestones.

His voice was slurred with the booze.

"I have been celebrating with Michael O'Hara and Stanislaus in the pub. They have joined Felix and bought a present to celebrate our wedding anniversary."

He took a swig of ale from a metal flask in his pocket.

"Guess what."

"A night on the town to see Felix perform? That would be a treat."

"No way. It wouldn't fill your tummy for years to come. They have bought us a large plot of waste land and a wooden hut, near the abattoir. They say it was dirt cheap. Father Thomas told them it was for sale. There's a pig sty with a boar and a sow they have nicknamed Jonathan and Maria."

His wife was gobsmacked.

He chuckled.

"We are landowners. We have our own smallholding with the mum and dad pigs and nine little piglets. There is enough land for an allotment and chickens. Cocks and hens! Eggs and bacon! Pork and onions for the rest of our lives."

"That would be wonderful! I can't believe it's true."

She sang, "This little piggy went to market, this little piggy stayed home. This little piggy ate roast beef, this little piggy had none. This little piggy went wee-wee-wee-weee, all the way home."

"We could flog some food on the market."

Jonathan took Maria's hand. "Come with me to inspect our new estate."

Lucia was awake now and trotted behind them down the alleyway towards Lambeth Palace.

They came to a strip of waste land. Two great big saddleback pigs ran grunting through the undergrowth, followed by nine piglets. The pig sty lay nearby.

"The O'Haras have asked carpenters to build us a wooden cabin. We should be able to move into our new home in a month or two."

He kissed Maria and Lucia cried out, "I want to kiss a piggy!"

"What shall we call our house?"

"The Kelly Pig Sty."

"I think there is a cow shed at the far end of the garden, behind the pig sty."

Maria laughed.

"We might take enough money on the market to buy our own cow. That would be wonderful, fresh milk and butter. Lucia could be our dairy-maid."

The little one was dancing up and down.

"You must always remember to pull the udders on opposite sides, darling."

"I don't understand. What's a nudder, Mummy?"

"Don't worry about that just yet. I expect it's a long way off."

They made their way home to celebrate with tea and bread and dripping. The chicken soup and potatoes were burned, as black as night.

Over the years the Kellys had acquired a mattress, a broken down table and two wooden chairs. Lucia balanced on a footstool. They were all gifts from Felix, the Golden Boy.

Maria clasped Jonathan's hand.

Lucia was prattling all the way home.

"I heard an old man say 'Home, James, and don't spare the horses.' It sounds cruel to the animals, I wonder what he meant?"

"It's only another way of saying 'Hurry home, James.'"

"A woman on the street corner said, 'I saw him in the pub last night. He was as dead as a do-do.' What's a do-do, Daddy?"

"It's a bird. I think they have been extinct for several hundred years."

"My friend Mary says she is a love-child. Am I a love-child?"

The father guffawed.

"You really are a silly little girl. You know how much we love you, but it's not quite the same."

"One of Stanni's books told me 'You can't make a silk purse out of a sow's ear.'"

"That is one thing we shan't be trying to do. Now for Heaven's sake be quiet, child, until we get home for our high tea."

The three Kellys, Jonathan, Maria and Lucia, walked hand in hand down the river path. The little one tried to copy a dance she had seen brother Felix rehearse, but fell flat on her bum.

She scrambled to her feet, ran off, picked a great big bunch of dandelions and gave them to Mummy.

She made a little garland and crowned herself with a tiara. In the meantime the Ma and Da had found a broken-down bench and his wife lay her head on his shoulder.

"What do you want, Daddy?" He was kissing his wife's pink cheeks.

Lucia snapped off a pretty yellow flower, ran across the path and tucked it into the collar of his shirt. Jonathan bellowed. "You little monkey. A damn great thorn pricked my throat."

"You know I am learning Botany at St Patrick's School; some people call it Nature Studies. The dandelions I gave Mummy were named after the French, *dent du lion*. That means *'tooth of the lion'*, so he might be biting you now.

"Look at all those lovely colours, white, blue and gold. The maidenhair fern has dark stems, light leaves and feathery fronds. Forget-me-nots were named in France – *Ne m'oubliez pas*.

Wet the bed is a strange name; I don't know where that comes from. It sounds rude, but they are only little white daisies."

These would border their new land, it was unbelievable. Stanislaus and Felix had created a miracle.

Jonathan said, "You are a clever kid. How on earth do you remember all those different names and where they come from?"

"They are in one school book, Daddy. Some people call forget-me-nots 'scorpion grass'. They teach us French at school. I know that *eau-de-vie* means 'water of life'."

Jonathan murmured, "It is the water of death for many men. There is a yellow Dutch liqueur made from egg yolks and brandy. Some alchos have strange ideas."

Suddenly Maria burst into tears; it was the thought of their little Rosa. She would love to live in a pig sty. Every piglet would have been given a name of its own. Nine Irish saints' names were ticking over in Maria's head now. In the child's favourite story, *Alice in Wonderland*, the queen's baby became a pig.

Maybe, in Rosa's mind, every piglet would have been a baby.

Oh, my God, an orphanage in a cow-shed, thought Maria.
Jonathan said, "Let's rejoice in this wonderful day. We shall soon be alone together; the only child at home when we move will be Lucia.

"Danny and Teresa are in Ireland; Felix is working his socks off in the theatre, living in an apartment with his manager. Lucia is a clever little girl, longing to teach poor kids. Father Doyle has promised to help her in a year or two. She may go to a university in England or in Dublin. It will be a new life. I will make a sign saying 'Kelly's Pig Sty'. I am sure Stanislaus will paint a picture of the animals."

"Cheeky little minx!" and he pretended to slap Maria's bum with his walking stick.

Maria laughed. "Be careful, Jonathan, I think that might be called assault and battery. You know we've got the Metropolitan Police in London now, so many laws are changing."

"I'll dot you one as well if you get too chatty."

They reached the hovel at last, ate a stale picnic, blew out the candles and made love on the wooden floor.

Lucia pretended to be asleep, but she was dreaming of Irish fairy stories; leprechauns and magic in the hills of Kerry. A letter from brother Danny in Dublin told her wonderful stories about Phoenix Park and the wild animals: giraffes, elephants and tigers. Lucia was longing to ride a camel; some of them had two humps. She wanted to hear the lions roar, trying to protect their babies from men. If the family worked hard in the Pig Sty they might be able to afford a summer holiday beside the Liffey. Teresa had invited the three of them any time they were free and could afford a break. Maybe in the school holidays?

Lucia had talked to Stanislaus and he promised her pocket money. She was sure they would be able to make the break.

Next year, maybe?

Maria tripped over a tussock of rough grass.

She gazed down and saw the mouth of a rabbit hole and remembered, once again, the life and death of Rosa in Wonderland. Her little girl.

Was she a heap of bones, a skeleton lying in some foul burial ground, or an angel floating in the sky?

She must talk to Father Doyle about the soul and spirit of her child, and to Stanislaus about Rosa's short life in this world.

How she would have loved the pig sty, playing with the animals and the birds; feeding a puppy-dog with scraps of food left-over at meal-times. Sleeping in a warm little cabin and eating two or three meals a day. Pork pies, fish from the river, Mummy's chocolate puds. Fruit and vegetables from the waste ground, now a kitchen garden on the Kelly estate.

Maria blew a kiss to the sky, the sun was fading.

"What on earth are you doing, Mummy? Have you got cold fingers? You can wear my woolly gloves."

They were trotting back home to celebrate with glasses of ale and lemonade.

Maria said, "Tonight I will read you a bedtime story called *Alice in Wonderland*." She had always kept a ragged book of fairy stories although she was never a great reader; time and incentive were lacking.

"You know I love stories about animals – cats and mongrel dogs. You often meet them on the street afterwards." She jumped up and down. "I'm going to be a teacher when I grow up. I'm going to be a teacher!"

Jonathan overheard the little one.

"I'm afraid you'll have to wait a year or two, ducky."

"If I am your baby girl, Daddy, you can carry me home."

Jonathan said to Maria, "Can you imagine a life with money? We shall even be able to spend a few nights wandering round the pubs together. These days the gin palaces have gas lighting and plate glass windows. Rum shrub is rum served with lemon and sugar. Gin, known as Mother's Ruin, is still a penny a glass. Even now I can buy the odd drink without having kittens when I learn the price. You might be excited by cage-fighting – two men lashing out at one another. They may be naked, I don't know if it's really wrestling or fighting."

"I don't give a damn; it sounds like a form of suicide. I would be so sorry for all the animals; everything sounds like a crazy obsession."

"You may be happy to eat revolting food like tripe. The idea of the pale slimy stomach of a cow, or venison, the flesh of a deer, makes me feel sick."

Maria shuddered and stroked her tummy.

They could hear the crow of the rooks in the roof of their hovel.

That night Maria lay dreaming of their new way of life in a log cabin: privacy, candleglow, no cockroaches, crickets or bugs scuttling across the ceiling: no fleas to nip her legs and lice in the hair. A life of luxury. Everything would be as clean as a whistle for the first time in years.

Jonathan cuddled his wife on their straw bed and she whispered, "Remember I don't want another baby, but we can still make love, I shall always love you. Good night, my Lord and Master."

They lay clasped in one another's arms while Lucia was fast asleep on the floorboards.

Maria said, "I can remember a few Irish poems and ballads but only one in English, 'I wander, lonely as a cloud'. I think it was written by William Wordsworth."

When their wooden cabin was built in two or three months' time, chickens would roost in the loft. Jonathan would wobble up a ladder to collect eggs or a bird for their Sunday supper.

A black and white cow would kip in the shed.

They were all gifts from Michael O'Hara and Felix.

Starvation was no longer a threat; it would be a life of luxury.

Weeks later Flossie-Bang-Bang sat on the window-sill of Kelly's Pig Sty gazing across the Southwark landscape at Lambeth Palace and the Thames. She might take flight, searching for bird seed or stale soda bread. She had escaped from the burial ground and lay for months in a cardboard box with Rosa's old bedroom slippers. Her striped wings twitched and she wanted to cry.

One day another little girl might love her. She remembered Lucia and began to dream.

Her sharp claws scratched the woodwork and splinters flew in the air.

She saw a tortoise treading very slowly across the grass, moving his head gently from side to side. Flossie-Bang-Bang flew down; she fancied a ride on his back. If he were naughty and tried to tumble her she would bite his little ears with her brown beak. It would be her first game since the loss of her darling Rosa, when they rode on the death cart with Father Doyle and the little girl went to another world. The birdie was free at last. The Kellys had unpacked their clutter, she might even watch them making love in their first posh double bed.

It might even give her ideas, to mate with a cock robin.

It was nearly bedtime and Maria and Lucia were talking.

"I will give you a big basket; a trug. You can sit outside the garden gate and sell some of the fruit and veg from the garden. I suppose they might fetch a penny each? I have found gooseberry bushes and some rhubarb. There are strawberries too and lots of wild flowers. If we pick a few at a time I will make bouquets for weddings and posies for wakes."

Maria was tearful for a moment, remembering her darling little Rosa, but tried to pull herself together.

"You might be able to collect quite a lot of money, with a great big basket of fruit and veg."

Lucia sat outside the garden gate for several days and beamed at every passer-by but she could not attract a single customer.

Then an old crone bought a few cherries and was so delighted with their sweet taste that she told all her friends.

Every afternoon, after school, a little queue lined up outside the Pig Sty.

Lucia sat at the garden gate selling the family's home-grown fruit and veg.

One day she danced into the kitchen and gave her mummy a big hug.

"Look how much I've taken this afternoon."

She flashed six pennies under Maria's nose, on to the kitchen table.

Mummy said, "I think it's time we had a party. This weekend I shall invite Michael and Natasha O'Hara, Stanislaus and Felix. I'm only sorry that Danny and Teresa have gone back to Ireland, but I think they will soon be able to afford a holiday in England.

"I am sure Father Doyle will join us for a little picnic in the garden, although we can't compete with all the aristos who entertain him."

Six months later there was a house-warming party at the Pig Sty with the Kellys and the O'Haras. The log cabin was a wonderful luxury. A double bedroom upstairs overlooked the water. Downstairs there was a large living-room and a kitchen. One could wash out of sight in a big cupboard. Teresa had a secret plan: she had left a few ornaments and pieces of furniture in her dad's attic before sailing to Ireland after her marriage. A gift to the in-laws.

Michael O'Hara said, "Now I have lost your Danny as a docker I thought you might be interested, Jonathan?" Food, money, and a house near Bandyleg Walk and Lambeth Palace.

Jonathan said, "Thank God, I'm still as strong as a horse. That's the first offer of a steady job I've had in years. You can count on me – tomorrow."

The family had clubbed together and bought lashings of food and drink on the market.

Maria said, "This is our first step up the ladder. You might become a wharfinger, my love."

Several years later his dream came true.

★★★

Felix was delighted with Auguste as his manager; he was honest and ambitious.

One evening he said, "A very wealthy American saw you perform. He loved the act and has offered to pay if you will tour the States for two or three weeks. I think he is one of the Rothschilds and they are all stinking rich. He is willing to cover all the travel expenses for you and your dresser, good hotels and luxury food. Plus a very generous salary."

Auguste grinned. "There would be an excellent percentage for me."

"Give me a day or two to make up my mind, Auguste. I prefer to travel with other performers. It would be bloody lonely, hundreds of miles away from family and friends."

Auguste sighed, "It would be a great step up the ladder, Felix. I will be patient and wait for you to decide."

The boy had already performed in Dublin, Cork and

Kildare, and spent a few days with Daniel, Teresa and the little 'uns.

Felix did not want to leave Ireland where so many were longing for a free country, but he would never be a politician in a million years – a Liberator, like Daniel O'Connell.

If he should ever decide to stay in Erin he would only be a song and dance man in the pubs, maybe Waterford Hall and the odd fair.

That's Entertainment!

A few weeks later the star and his fan were together in the dressing-room, nibbling a snack after the show. Felix sat in a low upholstered chair pretending to be casual. Colleen was perched on a high wooden stool.

Suddenly she jumped on to his lap and whispered, "Cuddle me. I am almost young enough to be your baby."

"You make me sound like an exhausted old man."

"Don't be daft, I am only joking."

Felix said, "You know I have been offered a short tour of the States. You could come with me and we might even find your father."

Colleen looked aghast. She whispered, "It's a lovely idea but I'm not sure I should travel alone with you. I might get into trouble."

Felix laughed. "I think that is a compliment, darling, unless yu are thinking of the Yankee gangs."

He signed the contract and they sailed to the States. Felix gazed out of his cabin window and saw the giant figure of a woman towering over the bay: The Statue of Liberty. She held a torch aloft in one hand, in the other lay a book, inscribed 4th July 1776.

Someone had told Felix this was a gift from the French nation; maybe it was to celebrate America's fight against the English.

It was high time for him to dress and be ready to disembark with his entourage.

His agent, Auguste, had arranged digs for them in Manhattan; two single rooms and a double for the dresser and his wife, the chaperones of the Irish virgin, Colleen.

Manhattan, a borough of New York, was bordered by the Hudson, East River, New York Bay and Harlem. He knew the cultural heart of the city included Broadway, Wall Street and Greenwich Village. The little band of pros had been warned to avoid Harlem, the land of the "blacky-toppers".

"You might be robbed or murdered", yet they all loathed the idea of racism.

Everyone had heard of the mafia, that was another world; the colour of your skin was irrelevant. Most of the gangsters were Italian or American, often with a base in Sicily. Poverty-stricken hit-men would kill for a dollar.

Felix and Colleen left their hotel rooms and walked together down Broadway, hand in hand.

Theatreland.

The Irish Song and Dance Man entertained with ballads and wallops and some of the latest tunes from the English cabarets and music-halls. He even worked one or two numbers he learned in Paris, on his tour with Stanislaus.

Colleen lurked in the dressing-room or the front row of the stalls.

The next date was Las Vegas. They would stay in The Venetian Hotel overlooking the lake and swim in the cool waters. Felix dreamed of a new life with the girl.

One of the Yankee stage hands asked the dresser and his wife, "How old is that pretty little girl who is travelling with you and Felix. Is she his bit of crumpet?"

"No way. I don't think either of them has ever had it off.

My wife would lay a bet they will marry when we go back to England. I was talking to the priest about under-age weddings and I think he said it went up from ten to twelve a few years ago. I believe it's fourteen now. The young lady told my wife she had the curse ages ago; she might have kids quite early."

"So many Yanks have told me they fancy her."

"They had better keep off. My boss has had fencing lessons and he can get quite mobile with his fists. They might get a punch in the gob. Tell them not to get any funny ideas of rape or stalking. Felix paid us to come over and act as her chaperones. We are both old enough to be her parents; a respectable man and wife.

"I understand the little one's father is somewhere in the States and she is longing to find him. They lost touch when he became a stowaway.

We have had a great time, living in posh hotels, seeing Manhattan, Broadway and the Statue of Liberty. I wonder whether we shall ever build a monument like that in Dublin, celebrating a free Ireland?"

He changed the subject. "I know Felix has been offered dates in Las Vegas and Los Angeles."

His wife broke into the conversation at last.

"I think that means 'The Angels' in Spanish. Colleen might become a ballerina. I have seen her rehearsing entrechats and arabesques in the dressing-room. She exercises at the barre using the towel rail in her bathroom. One day in the future they could work a double act on Broadway."

Felix laughed when he remembered his first visit to the theatre as a little boy. He told Colleen the story of his antics at the Elephant and Castle.

Now they rode together on the street railways of New York, that had been introduced in 1864. In 1889 a branch line was built between Times Square and the Kingsbridge Line. They

had a wide area to explore, learning about American history. There were so many stories about different nationalities and religions.

Broadway had been a one-way street and there were many fine old buildings, and The Winter Garden Theatre. This was too grand to invite him as a performer so the two young ones applauded from the stalls.

The various beliefs were obvious. The Presbyterian Hospital lay on Broadway. The Bloomingdale Road passes the Campus of Columbia University.

The young couple saw the Gothic Quadrangle of the Union Theological Seminary: Broadway City College and some fine hardstones face a landscaped garden. There were so many things they had never heard of in their school days. The Western Road was paved and widened during the nineteenth century and it was called Le Boulevard. In 1868 there was another plan for an arcade railway.

The young couple discovered that Broadway was the boundary between Greenwich Village and the East Village. New York University lies near Washington Square Park and there are many theatres. Bloomingdale Lunatic Museum existed from 1808 but moved later in the century. There was a Manhattan School of Music and education for the Jews.

Felix and Colleen were warned not to wander into Harlem; they might be in danger from the black community. Racism was rife in certain areas but the two young people would never be culpable. Thank God!

They both wanted their own life in Theatreland. England, Ireland and the States. Anywhere in the wide world. A dream life, together.

Felix and Colleen talked about everything under the sun; their families, the birth of Lucia and the death of his little sister Rosa.

Colleen's father had sent her to a school for girls in Dublin. Her mother had worked for a while behind the bar of a good hotel, but she was shot dead by an English soldier in a brawl. He was able to escape "justice" and bolted to Glasgow.

"The danger in America seems to be the mafia. I have met one of the Mafioso," and Felix told her the sad story of his gift from Federico. It was packed in his luggage when he was on his travels.

"Oh God! I hope my Daddy has found work. I know he would rather starve than be a gangster. He went to the Catholic University in Dublin; I suppose that might help a little. We shall never find him in this huge country; he might be living out on the prairie."

The American press had adopted Felix, the song and dance man, and scribbled some wonderful reviews.

Colleen lay on her hotel bed, daydreaming. One day Felix might ask her to marry him, when she was a mature woman?

Thank God, she would never become "one of the girls".

That night they left the theatre, hand in hand. There was a long queue, begging for autographs and handshakes.

In the dressing-room Colleen had said, "I am longing to see my daddy again. He may not believe I was too late to board the coffin ship. You know I never wanted to be alone in England."

That night a tall, dark man with iron-grey hair and violet eyes came forward after the show.

"Daddy, Daddy! It's the Da. How on earth did you find me? This is Felix."

"I know, darling. I am working as a journalist and there were pictures of you both in the theatre column."

Felix said, "Good evening, Sir. I am so happy to meet you. Shall we have a drink in the bar along the road? Tomorrow we go to Las Vegas where I am playing in cabaret. We may not meet again for a while. Do come with us if you can spare the time, I know Colleen would hate to lose sight of you quickly."

They strolled along the road together.

The waiter bowed from the waist and led them to a quiet corner table.

"Good evening, Mister Felix. It is so good to see you. The boss man saw you enter and wishes to offer a glass of sherry, on the house. Which do you prefer, dry or sweet? I think I can guess what the young lady will choose.

He balanced the tray of drinks in mid-air and performed a little pirouette.

"I, too, was a dancer, Mr Felix, but I never made the grade. My wife and I saw you the other night, Sir. It was fantastic!"

The man took a deep breath. "May I take your order now?"

Felix, Colleen's father, said to Sean "I must be careful what I eat. I dare not put on weight."

The waiter was standing at his elbow with the menu.

"We have some fresh salmon, crab salad, a quiche and a delicious beef stew."

Felix chose a bottle of bubbly. Meanwhile Sean was having a great time chatting with the daughter he had not seen for months on end.

"There are so many nationalities and languages in the States. That has helped me find work as a journalist." He turned to Felix. "Be careful when you are working in Las Vegas; it is a motley crew. Remember that old quote about Lord Byron? 'Mad, bad and dangerous to know.'"

Meanwhile the waiter came to the table with a pale pink rose.

"A present for you, milady. One lovely flower to another." Colleen blushed.

Felix spoke. "I have a question, Sir, if you can spare us the time. May I ask Colleen if she will marry me? Do I have your permission, Sir?"

Father Sean gave a broad smile and nodded his iron-grey head.

"Yes, my boy. I think she is a very lucky girl. I know she has found an honourable, talented young Irish man."

Colleen was smiling behind a snow-white hanky.

Felix fell to one knee on the plush carpet of the bar.

"Colleen. Will you marry me when we sail back to England? I love you."

"Yes, Felix, yes. I have been waiting for this moment. I love you more than life itself. I shall always love you."

He kissed her rosebud mouth.

Sean said, "Bless you, my children. May I announce your wonderful news in the theatre columns – they will cover New York, Los Angeles and Vegas. Angeles, the city of angels. I must go soon; otherwise I shall be asleep all day tomorrow."

Felix was thinking of Los Angeles, San Francisco and Sin City. The Golden Gate and Fisherman's Wharf.

"When I was a kid I only knew Southwark like the back of my hand, a street urchin. My life has changed, thank God, and I can say the same for my Ma and Da. They live in comfort for the first time in years. Kelly's Pig Sty is near Lambeth Palace, the home of the Archbishop of Canterbury. I have encountered your father, now I would love you to meet my family. People call my Da 'Old Chubby Chops', so you must not expect sophisticated glamour. Mother Maria is still beautiful, with long black hair streaked with silver, and a body that is as slim as a reed, after giving birth to four children.

"Will you come and meet my darling parents when we return to England? I am sure Father Doyle will be happy to marry us unless he is on a begging tour across Europe. You know I have been living away from home, in a Soho apartment house. There are four rooms, a kitchen and a bathroom." He kissed her rosy lips saying "One might be a nursery in the years to come."

She blushed.

"I might decide to stay at home with you and our babies."

"I could always make a living playing long seasons at Gatti's Under the Arches and the Lyric Theatre. I would never need to tour the world."

★★★

Gertrude, the chaperone lady, helped Colleen unpack her luggage. It had burgeoned on the journey with gifts from Felix and many new-found admirers.

The dresser and his wife were going to be in residence at the London apartment. The charming girl was happy to cope with all the domestic duties. She would enjoy playing with the youngster's wardrobe, washing and ironing. They had become good friends on the journey to America.

Gertie was an East Ender; her family lived in Stepney, near one of Dr Barnardo's homes. When she was a little girl she had dreaded the thought of being shipped to Canada, but she had survived in England and made the grade.

She met her darling husband in the library and they began talking about books.

Walter said, "My Granddad was a Scot so we all read Robert Burns and Walter Scott when we were growing up."

They were sitting together on a bench when he said, "I will read aloud to you."

Gertrude confessed she could scarcely read or write but she was longing to learn.

They fell in love, married, and her husband gave her lessons every afternoon.

They made love with joy but there were never any babies.

One day there might be a miracle, she was still in her early thirties.

★★★

Felix said, "I think we should catch an omnibus and walk over the bridge when we visit the family. If we arrive in a hansom cab they might think we were pretending to be grand."

Colleen chose a pale blue gown, a Paisley shawl and a lace bonnet.

"Let's go. I have put on my leather breeches." He laughed. "Father might slap my bum for deserting them."

The time had come. They set out in the hot sunshine so Colleen carried a French parasol to avoid sunstroke.

"This will be a big surprise. They are not expecting us."

"Perhaps you should have warned them in advance?"

"No way."

They had landed at Tilbury Docks and Felix hired a horse and carriage for the journey to West London. The money paid to him by the Yankees was out of this world.

"We shall be able to afford a trip to Ireland. Do you fancy a honeymoon in Dublin?"

"No thank you, darling. I want to be alone with you."

"We will go and meet the family for the first time, and my dear friend Stanislaus. He taught me so many things on our trip to Paris. How to avoid Free Love on the banks of the Seine, in the parks and in the brothels of Montmartre. Be my only love, darling, in this world and the next."

Colleen was amazed when she saw the apartment for the first time in her life. It lay between Holland Park and Kensington Palace – two double bedrooms, a guest room and a fabulous drawing-room. Colleen would sleep in the guest room for the time being.

Stanislaus had helped his friend Felix furnish the apartment. The walls of the living-room were lined with pictures and books, many about the theatre. They included Gustav Flaubert's *Madame Bovary*, Rudyard Kipling and Hans Christian Andersen's *Fairy Tales*. There were two pictures by Rosa Bonheur; toads kissing one another and birds on the nest.

A robin by Stanislaus raised its beak in the air.

"I think it's lovely, Felix. I shall never want to go out again."

She rhapsodised over his white double bed chamber.

"Of course we shall share it after our honeymoon."

Everything was as white as snow, apart from red roses on the eiderdown and a blue Venetian chandelier.

Felix kissed her passionately. "Tomorrow we will fix a date for our wedding in St George's."

"Come with me, darling," and she answered, "Anywhere, in the whole wide world."

Felix and Colleen pranced down the footpath towards the Pig Sty.

Maria caught sight of them through the kitchen window and called out, "Jonathan, Felix has come to see us at last."

She flung open the wooden door to greet her son.

He kissed her on both cheeks and shook hands.

"I thought Sunday was a good day to choose; you might both be at home. May I introduce my fiancée, Helena Colleen. We are hoping to meet Father Doyle when we leave here and fix a date for the wedding. Of course he may be on a begging tour across Europe. Don't worry; it won't be a grand affair. Colleen's father is living in the States, her mother died years ago. I know brother Danny, Teresa and the twins are living in Dublin, and Stanislaus is in World's End. He is sure to come."

The parents gazed in wonderment at this lovely little girl.

Maria thought, *I hope she's not in the family w*ay, but her tummy was as flat as a pancake.

Mother-in-law-to-be realised Colleen was an innocent who would never be "rolling in the hay" without a wedding ring.

The world was full of gropers, but not their Felix.

"I was just making a cup of tea. Will you join us in the garden?"

Felix laughed and put down his ruck-sack.

"I have brought us champagne to celebrate my lucky days."

Stanislaus promised to be best man at the wedding.

★★★

Silver candelabra, crystal glasses, bouquets of apricot roses and carnations graced the table on the stage of the South London Palace of Varieties.

Another debut. Auguste shivered with delight.

Smoked salmon with thin slices of lemon, caviar, roast beef and Yorkshire pudding, pasta dishes. Clam chowder – soup made from clams, salt pork, potatoes and onions. The menu went on and on; there was an endless choice.

Waiters served the guests.

A pussycat was the guest of honour at the wedding breakfast. She was an old, old black and white lady; one of Stanni's gifts to little Rosa before she died. La Madeleine was as elegant as the queen. She wore a frilly pink collar decorated with sequins and fake diamonds. The bride and groom had adopted the old lady and she lived a life of luxury. She could smell the fish and jumped out of her wicker basket on to Colleen's lap.

Over the years she had found a mate in one of the back alleys and he was named Beelzebub. "Bubby" was as white as a sheet with tortoiseshell paws but he was becoming a little rusty as the years went by. Sometimes he chose to sleep with Maria and Old Chubby Chops.

Who on earth had nicknamed him Beelzebub? It was the name of a fallen angel in John Milton's *Paradise Lost*.

The little devil was as good as gold, but today a paw grabbed a Whitstable oyster from a dish at the lower end of the table.

Felix stroked his whiskers saying, "You are a very naughty boy, Bubby."

The older Kellys had money to burn for the first time in their lives, and they bought a new wardrobe for their younger son's wedding.

The Da wore an embroidered satin waistcoat in emerald green, and tails.

Maria chose a lime green velvet gown and Lucia created her own pair of golden pants.

The fishmonger's daughter from Dublin was pushing her barrow across the square at Covent Garden singing, "Cockles and Mussels, alive alive-o!"

Two yobbos called out, "It's the tart with the cart!"

His mate bawled out, "She's doing a fart!"

The pretty girl came closer crooning, "She caught the favour and nothing could save her."

Sweet Molly Malone snatched two long wet fish from the barrow, slimy eels, and slapped the two boys round the face. It was the shock of their lives; they yowled.

"Enjoy your free dinner lads," and the crowd of onlookers roared with laughter.

Half an hour later she pushed the empty barrow home with a bag full of coppers tied to her hips.

Mum and Dad were over the moon and toasted the little one in "a drop of the black stuff" and Mother's Ruin.

Sweet Molly Malone swallowed a pork pie saying, "Good luck to the gutter-snipes."

Father Doyle's first illness was in 1864 when he was seventy-one years of age.

He wrote "St George's and cod liver oil. Sir, they have often called me oily-mouth. I am swimming in oil – only put a Lucifer match to me and I shall enlighten all the house and there will be a saving of gas – of which much is used in this establishment.

"The blister came in the evening, black and large, like a burnt pancake. It went on and kept on all night, and made marks that still remain."

In 1876 the Doctor wrote his final letter to *The Tablet*. He said Mass for the last time on 9th April 1879 in the Petre Chantry and for the soul of his old friend, the Hon Edward Petre.

He was unable to leave his room after nearly sixty years in the priesthood. On the 6th July he was sinking fast and surrendered his soul to God.

The vast cathedral in which the plaintive Placebo Domino in those solemn Vespers for the dead seems to be ringing in our ears. Eternal rest give to him, Our Lord, and let perpetual light fall on him.

When Father Doyle passed into another world there was a vast congregation in St George's Cathedral, among them the Provost's sister and about ninety of the clergy of Southwark and Westminster.

The Carrara marble statue in the vault represents Father Doyle in his vestments, his head supported by angels, and his feet resting on dragons.

He passed away at the ripe age of eighty-six, leaving an estate valued at £450.

Requiescat in Pace.